TO DEFEND, TO DESTROY

TO DEFEND

TO DESTROY

BY JAMES RESTON, JR.

W · W · NORTON & COMPANY · INC · NEW YORK

Published simultaneously in Canada by George J. McLeod Limited, Toronto

FIRST EDITION
Printed in the United States of America
Library of Congress Catalog Card No. 78-128036
SBN 393 08621 6
1 2 3 4 5 6 7 8 9 0

For Blake

TAIPEI

October 1967

I know that I shall meet my fate
Somewhere among the clouds above;
Those that I fight I do not hate,
Those that I guard I do not love:
My country is Kiltartan Cross,
My countrymen Kiltartan's poor,
No likely end could bring them loss
Or leave them happier than before.
Nor law, nor duty bade me fight,
Nor public men, nor cheering crowds,
A lonely impulse of delight
Drove to this tumult in the clouds;
I balanced all, brought all to mind,
The years to come seemed waste of breath,
A waste of breath the years behind
In balance with this life, this death.

—W. B. YEATS, "An Irish Airman Foresees His Death"

I

October 2, 1967

On a warm cloudless day in the autumn of 1967, the 11:53 train from Kaohsiung to Taipei moved into the lush valley of central Taiwan. The texture of the soil had begun to change from the sandy infertility of the southern terrain. Flooded paddies became more frequent, the lines of their borders conforming to the folds of verdant hills. Often the delineated ponds were dominated by a peasant behind a plodding water buffalo and a rudimentary plow, carving rich chunks of wet sod from the life-giving mother earth. The train was part of the daily routine and seemed to go unnoticed by the toiling peasants. As the train lumbered by, a man in a conical hat knelt in the mud, straddling a row of tender rice shoots. A parallel line on each side of the row extended from his toes to the border behind him, marking the path of his crawl through the mud as he tended gently to every shoot. A few feet away a woman bundled up against the intense rays of the sun struggled with a load of green vegetables stuffed into two bamboo baskets on either end of a carrying pole. The load must have been heavy —perhaps 40 catties to a basket—for she walked in short steps, heel and toe, like a competitor in a frantic walking race. Behind her on the packed-mud border of a neighboring paddy stood a young barefoot boy, no more than six or seven years old, in a yellow baseball cap and short khaki pants—rigid, straight, unflinching, saluting this awesome link between the distant Chinese cities.

It was odd that an American should have been on this

train. Along with the well-dressed businessmen and functionaries from Taipei and Kaohsiung, foreigners usually rode only the tourist trains, with their white napkined chairs and pert stewardesses. But in the rear car the young Caucasian hunched against the filmy window, his chin resting on his hand, dully watching the pastoral scenery flash before him like a travel movie. He was dressed in a drab, gray business suit and was crowded in by a family of five Chinese. Across from him the aging mother, her weathered face framed by a worn purple scarf, presided over her brood. Occasionally she glanced at the young man as if to make sure he was not making gestures toward her teenage daughter. In the next row of seats a group of Nationalist GIs in fading green fatigues and matching crushed hats played a boisterous game of cards.

The discomfort of the crowding and the noise and the stench of stale tobacco smoke showed in the expression on the American's face. He wished he could trust the plane, but the Nationalist DC-3s were notorious for their crashes. As the acrid haze became thicker and thicker, and one toothless GI gained a loud upper hand in the card game, the American crawled over his watchful seatmates and moved to the corridor between the two coaches. He sat down on a bundle of boxes wrapped in a large brown-and-black-striped cloth. At least it was not smoky there, though the clatter of the wheels on the tracks was greater than the clatter inside. Above the young man's head, bold white Chinese characters were set against a brilliant blue background: WORK HARD! PREPARE TO GO BACK TO THE MAINLAND!

The Westerner postponed going to the toilet as long as he could, for he knew what its condition would be. To his surprise, it was not too bad. About seven on a scale of ten. He took off his jacket, and after noticing that the door hook had been yanked off, hung the coat on the doorknob. As he sat down, his eye fell on the white envelope that protruded from the inside pocket. He took it out with the care that one handles a nestling.

The Chinese characters that flowed down the thin sheet of rice paper had a strong sweep to them. The American took out a pen and an old envelope and practiced writing some of the characters. He took pride in his ability to write these difficult figures. It had taken thousands of hours of practice to make his script indistinguishable from an Oriental's hand. His Chinese and Japanese friends were always impressed at his proficiency. But for some reason the simplest of all figures—the character for "mouth"—gave him trouble. It was a simple square, yet the Orientals had a special way of rounding off and slurring the last two strokes which the young man could not quite capture. It was a shame that the figure appeared so often as a component of complex characters.

He looked at the page for a character with a square in it. A man's personality comes through so much stronger in Chinese script than in English handwriting, he thought. A strong personality had written these characters.

Mr. James Baskins will help my father to return from the mainland for a family reunion. I agree to perform whatever he stipulates in return. In addition, it will be carefully observed that nothing will be said about this matter or the purpose of this trip.
Persons agreeing: Chuang Li Kwan
James Baskins

A sudden jerk of the train yanked the American out of his daze. They were slowing down for a station. The foreigner looked out the open slit in the opaque window. Tai Jung: 台中 The square in the characters seemed to be winking at him. He hurriedly organized himself and returned to his seat.

The train stopped with a lurch. The swarm of humanity

hovered around the train. The car hissed and heaved from side to side. Old ladies pushed toward the door as if they were in a scrum, their vocal cords exercising strange extremes. The din was tremendous.

Soon it was over and the train was under way again. The Westerner relaxed a bit. The disapproving family had gotten off. The journey was half over.

He returned to the corridor. As he did, he noticed an old man, bent with age, laboring up the aisle toward him from the next car. With one hand the octogenarian balanced himself with a cane, and with the other he held a bamboo birdcage ahead of him at the curve of his worn frame. In the cage were four furry yellow ducklings. The American marveled at the face, so wrinkled that the eyes and mouth were no more than prominent lines in a complex mosaic. The young man reached to open the corridor door for the old gentleman.

"Speak Mandarin?" The old man formed his words deliberately, as he slowly placed his cage in the corridor and strained to look up into the American's face. The American saw the suggestion of an eyeball for the first time.

"Ssu."

"Is this yours? I noticed you were in the toilet before me." The old man groped beneath the folds of his brown shawl and slowly took out the white envelope containing Chuang's contract. "You pay a little reward for me finding it?"

Feeling faint, the American fumbled in his pocket. "Why . . . yes . . . of course . . . here, take this twenty New Taiwan dollars."

"Thank you. You should be more careful next time, young man." The wrinkles around his eyes lengthened in what was probably a condescending smile. The old man extended his crooked hand for the money and deposited it in the hidden chest pocket. The American fumbled to help him with his cage, muttering more feeble words of thanks. Without acknowledging them, the old man turned and scuffled painfully back down the passage.

The American slumped against the side of the train in relief and raised his eyes to the ceiling. He could see his message to TONTO now:

OPERATION JONAH COMPROMISED BY 80-YEAR OLD CHINAMAN WITH BIRD CAGE. REGRETS. BARTLETT

He returned to his seat. Cramped between a new set of stoic companions, he looked even odder now, like a Charles Addams character, with a big smile on his face. It was all he could do to keep from laughing out loud.

II

October 15, 1966

Nearly a year before that dangerous train ride began, Jonathan Bartlett, aged twenty-seven, single, still none the worse for wear after a year and a half in the Army, had been happy enough ensconced in his obscure glassed-in cubicle in the Pentagon. His work was not uninteresting—he assisted in a project on battlefield television, looking to the day when commanders could run their battles surrounded by television sets—and he occasionally saw reports which reflected the true state of affairs in Vietnam. Lt. Bartlett enjoyed his secret knowledge and thought it would be useful after the Army in some academic program he might take up.

The Pentagon had for Lt. Bartlett the virtue of size. He welcomed his invisibility among the scores of field-grade and general officers who populated the halls, and coordinated the contingency plans for two major wars and one minor war at any given time. With such problems to deal with, no one had much time for Bartlett's military appearance—a pleasant switch from OCS and advanced training.

To begin with, he was not particularly attractive. His face was square and his chin strong, but this symmetry was coarsened by a nose that was too large and eyes that were too small and close together. When he looked at himself in the mirror, he decided that his wide mouth that broke easily into a broad smile was the nicest feature of his face. If he were ever to be physically attractive, he concluded, it would have to be in old age with a distinguished, wise look.

In uniform he often looked like the old rag man. He was continually neglecting a thumb mark or a rain spot on his military brass or a scuff mark on his shoes. In OCS his oversights were often attributable to his practice of performing his military duties to Vivaldi. His gray military glasses always seemed to rest slightly askew on his nose. And he had always liked long hair. In his college days at Ohio State, his sandy brown hair had swept across a narrow forehead and curled upwards just above his thin eyebrows. He liked the notion that it made him look English. Often he wore a heavy turtleneck sweater that extended below his buttocks and a pair of thick German corduroys that were cleaned, it was said, by brushing the dirt into the crevices between the wide cords. In this costume Bartlett would feel himself ready for an evening of beer and cream-cheese sandwiches at Zach's Delicatessen with the other intellectuals.

In the military Bartlett attempted a compromise. Around his ears, he kept his hair clipped closely, short enough to provoke a colonel's disapproving look only now and then. On the top of his head, however, his hair stayed almost as long as it had always been. The difference was that on military occasions he slicked down his hair in a manner completely inappropriate to the configurations of his face, and on social occasions he washed and teased it to look healthy and windblown. The technique worked in neither situation for in both he looked disheveled.

His orders had read simply: "Reassignment to Headquarters, 243rd Special Activities Group, Sword Island, Hawaii, pending further orders." The grapevine had it that he was bound for a special assignment. But early on Bartlett had learned to discount rumors. In the Army a special assignment could mean anything from scraping the grease pits to photographing a colonel's poodle. And at least it was not Vietnam.

But the young lieutenant had other reasons for dismay; months before he had heard in detail about his new unit, and the reports had not been encouraging. The source of information had been Lt. Ray Rolland, a blond, balding, amusing friend from Wyoming, who had struggled with Bartlett through OCS and advanced training, and had then been sent to the 243rd when Bartlett went to the Pentagon. But Rolland had lasted only two months in the 243rd before volunteering for Vietnam; a month later he was under cover in Hue.

At first Bartlett could not conceive of his friend's tribulations in the 243rd, which Rolland relayed in his letters. Bartlett would always remember Rolland as the wry upstart who nearly washed out of OCS for cussing out a platoon sergeant. After a drunken evening at the Benning Bunny Hop, Rolland was awakened at 5:30 by the platoon sergeant's usual morning greeting, always delivered with the delicacy of a soundtruck.

"Alright, you fuckin' bums, hit the deck."

Rolland lept out of his top bunk and in front of his hundred baymates shouted close into the startled sergeant's face, "*I'VE HAD FIFTEEN YEARS OF CATHOLIC EDUCATION AND YOU CAN'T TALK TO ME THAT WAY!*"

Rolland visited the stockade for that, and would never admit to anyone, even when he was drunk, whether the outburst had been spontaneous, or whether it had been secretly planned the night before.

Bartlett had reread Rolland's first letter from the 243rd as he tidied up his cubicle in the Pentagon for the last time.

Dear Jon,

If life could be pleasant by just living in nice places this would be bliss. I'm living in a pad which has a spectacular view of Pearl. It's high in Halawa Heights, and in the evenings I come home, pour myself a martini, and then watch the show from the brilliant orange sunset over Waianae Range, to the big ships coming into Pearl below me with their flags flying, then over to Hickam Field where the Phantoms and cargo planes take off for Nam at dusk. It's really a beautiful sight. I bet the brass living above me on the hill are sipping their martinis too, and hankering after the days of World War II when the military ran these islands as totally as the half naked kings and queens of Hawaii did a hundred years before.

Sometimes I have one of the girls over from the Marine Corps women's barracks at Camp H.M. Smith. That's the Marine base up the hill named for General H.M. Smith. The story goes that H.M. stands for "Howling Mad," a nickname he was supposed to have gotten at Corregador, when he boomed over the loudspeaker from his easychair on board a carrier: "AW RIGHT, YOU MARINES, GET OFF YOUR FUCKIN ASSES AND HIT THAT BEACH."

The girls from the barracks talk the same way sometimes, and so I sometimes use the same approach. I outrank most of em anyway. There's a story about one floating around who likes to screw in a dumpster. I guess it's hard to find privacy up there.

From up here at dusk, Sword Island—that's the island in Pearl where the 243rd is—looks beautiful, but don't be fooled. Things change in the stark light of day. The unit's mission is "to plan and launch covert operations against Communist-held areas of the Far East." That sounds more awesome than it is. The 243rd has so few operations that there isn't much planning and executing going on. North Vietnam and China are the main targets, but nobody, not even CISCO, is very successful in getting info on China. And what little we're getting on North Vietnam is no help to commanders in Nam who need 20 bombing targets a day to keep their sorties up.

Of course, there is OPlan B300. It's the best thing the 243rd has on North Vietnam. The source in Hanoi keeps reporting the imminent collapse of North Vietnam. Col. Dean Shannon, the commander of the unit, knows this is the intelligence the President wants to hear, so the operaion is retained. It's good publicity for the unit.

Col. Shannon considers himself the finest of the old wrap-leg infantry. He is *the 243rd.* L'unit, c'est moi. *The sputtering life of the unit comes from his decaying personage. But he's dangerous, cause he's afraid, if you can believe it, not of war or of his superiors but, God help him, of being passed over. It's already happened twice and that means he gets one more chance. Can you guess why he's so afraid of not making general? He doesn't have a college education! Ha. The new modern Army has passed him by. That's why he's so rough on me. "You college punks think you can run my job and my execs at the same time better than we can. I'll show you a few things before you're out of here." He actually told me that on our first meeting.*

Anyway, since Col. Shannon probably is *going to be passed over, the Pentagon did him a favor several years ago. The 243rd had been in Japan for 10 years, but in 1964 radical students over there made it dangerous to continue operations. So Shannon pleaded with his friends in Washington to relocate to Sword Island. I guess an island all his own appealed to the old fart's imagination. So he got his plum.*

In practice Sword Island has been less than a total blessing for Shannon. Rather than adding prestige to the 243rd, officers at the Club joke about King Shannon of Whore Island and the beautiful and dangerous women who dance for the court before being sent to the field as intelligence agents. And the enlisted men who live on "the rock" are giving Shannon a hell of a time. A near riot ensued last week when rats were seen crawling the walls of the Quonset hut that serves as enlisted men billets. Some of these guys feel that if they have to live under combat conditions they might as well be paid for it. They volunteer for Vietnam and are soon gone. The others simply stew in their discontent, take it out on their buddies, and develop that peculiar sneer of the military man that outsiders mistake for physical toughness. Were the enemy smart, he would approach some of these poor souls. Many have access to important material. Perhaps the enemy isn't interested.

Anyway, Shannon tries to frighten his men into line. In one session of greeting new men, he approached a corporal with a college education who was filing documents.

"Do you like your job?" he asked.

"Well, sir . . ."

"Do you have any choice?" And the colonel went on to the next man.

Then there was the time the supply room door wasn't open when it should have been. Shannon kicked it in. Or the time the trash can wasn't emptied on time. Shannon threw it out the second story window.

So the men of the 243rd live in mortal fear of 'Big Dean' and Big Dean likes it that way. But the men are not the only ones he tries to buffalo. For example, he took a visiting Japanese general to a mountain overlook behind Honolulu several weeks ago, pointed out the pass in the Waianae Mountains through which the Japanese planes flew on Dec. 7, 1941, and boasted how he would have done it differently had he been in command. . . .

Bartlett absorbed all this in that obscure corner of his brain reserved for military matters. He was happy that the Army was a temporary indiscretion of his, lasting only several years, and that he did not have to shudder before such idols as this Col. Shannon.

Not long after the first letter, Bartlett got another from Rolland, saying that Shannon had made it impossible for him, and that he too was volunteering for Vietnam. Bartlett was not surprised at Rolland's move, but his reasons were disturbing. Besides the situation with Shannon, he had mentioned the benefits of Vietnam duty: the extra-combat pay (all tax free), the privileges (with a story of a friend who had built an opera library through the PX while in Vietnam), the choice of a stateside assignment upon return. He even mentioned the free postage from the combat zone. How silly, Bartlett thought.

November 1, 1966

Lt. Bartlett decided to take a thirty-day leave before shipping out to Hawaii. There was no telling what would happen to him there or where he might be sent on further orders. He was nervous about the future. Could this be a Vietnam assignment after all? He hated the uncertainty. Perhaps he should volunteer for Vietnam like Rolland. That at least would remove this grating anxiety, but at most it might . . . No, he had best ride this one out.

The month at home would be a pleasant time. Bartlett loved Cleveland in the fall. It meant cocktail parties in Shaker Heights and touch football, hunting at Uncle Bill's on the lake and trysting in a pile of oak leaves. Bartlett planned his visit so that it would end after Thanksgiving—a holiday when he knew Maria would come home from Berkeley.

It had been a year since he had seen Maria Hemmings. She had gone off to California, flushed with pride at her graduation with honors at the University, and excited about her deeper studies in Oriental art to come. Her letters had overflowed with enthusiasm about the joys of the Bay Area, about camping and skiing, new friends and campus demonstrations. In one letter to Bartlett she had enclosed a clipping from the San Francisco *Chronicle*. The photo showed Maria, in a bikini, chained to an oak tree and smiling coquettishly at a burly disapproving workman with a saw in hand. Underneath, the caption read "Radical Conservationists Protest Tree Cutting for Parking Lot."

Bartlett smiled as he watched these interests develop. He had been responsible for them. She had been so fresh and innocent when they first met in Columbus—he a senior and she a sophomore. He had been taken by the delicate lines of her smooth, olive face, her high cheek bones and finely shaped nose, her deep brown eyes and tousled amber hair, her long lithe body. But her beauty alone had not been enough to keep him interested—particularly once he had possessed it—for he fancied himself a rebel in those days. He scoffed at her straight Episcopalian background out of boredom, took her to political discussions, badgered her about her indifference to social issues. He had watched her confusion grow in faint amusement, but when she told him one Sunday that she had been unable to take communion and was leaving the church, he realized that it had been an unfair game. He introduced her to Oriental art after that, partly out of a feeling of guilt over what he had destroyed. She had loved it. Now, no doubt, she knew much more than he.

In the two years after college when he taught elementary school, agonizing over a decision about the military and waiting for Maria to finish college, their relationship glowed with intensity. They had fought and loved with equal zest, but there had always been a basic understanding between them. Maria had poured herself out to him, buoying him up in his high, incredibly high, periods of joy when he was a spirited child. And she stayed by his side in his fuming silent depressions when he became a tyrant to her—helping, urging, joking, trying to rescue him from himself.

Those awful moods had loomed more often as Bartlett approached his induction into the Army, and Maria had found her task more difficult. For in a quiet way she had come to believe that all young men were obligated to resist involvement in the war—a notion that *he* had implanted in her head. When he finally went into the Army, she was deeply disappointed. She felt that she had been taken for granted, that he had not only run out on her but mocked her abhorrence of the war as well. She had done her best not to show her disappointment that last night when they had driven to the dunes and made love long and sweetly on the sand. She knew he was nervous and frightened too.

In the first three weeks of his leave, Lt. Bartlett asked himself why he had come home. The pace of life was too slow, too even, somehow too civilized. He could not relate to it. His pattern of life seemed to have broken down. He moped around the house, read cheap novels late into the night and slept until noon, speculated about his next assignment with his nervous parents and went to foreign films. He could not motivate himself to seek out old classmates or even go to cocktail parties. Would Maria never get there? After a time his agitated mother took to badgering him about the midden of a room where he spent most of his time.

The week before Thanksgiving Lt. Bartlett went to his Uncle Bill's ranch on the lake for some bird hunting. Even that made him feel uncomfortable. He did not particularly like to hunt. Guns scared him. And now they reminded him of his humiliation on the firing range in Basic Training. He had put too much oil on his M-14 before the final test, and every time it fired, little oil droplets splattered across his glasses. His drill sergeant laughed like hell as he watched Bartlett quickly wipe off his right lens with a handkerchief after each shot. "How'd you do," the grinning sergeant asked Bartlett as the trainee climbed out of the foxhole with filmy glasses. Bartlett replied with an indistinguishable hiss.

No, Bartlett did not like to kill birds. They'd never done anything to him.

The day before Thanksgiving finally came, and Maria arrived in Cleveland. Bartlett might have expected an exchange of telegrams on her arrival time, and a passionate reunion at the airport. Instead Maria simply called the Bartlett household after she arrived and had visited with her parents for a few hours. They agreed to meet after dinner, but Maria set the condition that she be home early.

She looked stunning that night. The West Coast had taught her to accentuate her natural beauty. Her hair was longer, and no makeup marred her face. She wore a simple loose shift with squiggly lines and a blue rebozo. Her bearing conveyed the instinctive freedom of a woman without pretension or guile.

They got along well that evening after their first nervousness dissipated, though they talked at cross purposes—she about her new exciting world in Berkeley, he about his adventures and new orders. They drove out to an overlook by the lake, and he kissed her a few times and then took her home at midnight. They planned to drive out to the dunes the following day.

Bartlett spent Thanksgiving morning packing his duffle bag and getting his uniform in order. That would give him time to sleep the following morning before his flight to the coast and on to Hawaii. He floated in daydreams through these preparations and later through the huge meal and the toasts of good luck to him, his mind on Maria, on what he could say to her now, of whether he could propose to her now before she slipped away beyond reach into her new life on the coast.

Soon enough she was beside him in his parent's car, and they were on the way to the dunes, to the small pond behind the beach that they had discovered several summers before and where they had never seen another human being.

"Have you forgiven me for the time I slapped you out here?" he asked her haughtily.

"Certainly not."

Bartlett supposed that he raised the subject of their worst fight to see if Maria could smile about it now. Everything had to come out. He had to know what her memory of their relationship was—the hurt as well as the joy—to know if she still loved him enough to think about marriage. That dreadful incident had haunted him in his sleep many times in Washington.

At that time, some months ago, he had been in the Army only long enough to take a confused pride in his survival as a military man, and she had teased him about it.

"Go to *HELL!*" he had shouted at her, and flung his wine glass as far as he could. It landed with a muffled gurgle in the middle of the pond. "I don't have to put up with this every time I come back here!"

"You're acting like a baby."

"Fine comfort you are. I'm the one that's under pressure, not you. All you do . . ."

"That's not my fault. It was your choice."

"Choice!"

"Yes, choice. You wanted it. You needn't act as if you were victimized."

"Oh, you've been talking to your draft-dodging friends again. You have no more conception of . . ."

"Of your games. I should know better than anyone. You're a coward, Jon."

He had slapped her, and for a second they stood looking at one another in wide-eyed disbelief. And then he was kissing her reddened skin frantically, wildly, babbling apologies, as her body began to contort in a sob. That awful mistake . . .

"You'll never believe it was an accident, will you?" he ventured now.

"Well I did call you a coward right before you hit me."

"Maybe I did swing out of anger, but really, I was just trying to sting your shoulder a little."

"Well, your aim was pretty bad then."

"You had to duck into the trajectory."

Maria silently watched the buildings of the suburbs fly by. She offered no more information on the subject, and Bartlett did not pursue it.

In another hour the large car turned off onto a sandy dirt road with several abandoned shacks along the side. After half a mile the road widened and then abruptly ended in a clearing. Beyond, the expanse of Lake Erie stretched before them. The wind had begun to kick up off the lake, and swirls of sand spiraled on the white embankment ahead of them. A quiet, unbothered walk through the dunes to their pond suddenly seemed like a bad idea.

Maria looked to Bartlett for a decision.

"Let's try it anyway," he said, "we've come this far."

"If you say so," said Maria reaching for a scarf in her purse, "but remember, I'm no soldier."

They walked along the sandy pathway, through the small pines on the fringe of the beach, and then emerged into a range of huge dunes. The wind gusted with a modulated whine above them, and as they would pass from the protection of a hillock, the sand lashed against them, stinging their faces, penetrating their clothing, covering their shoes like a trail of snow. Beyond the whitecaps across the lake a dark mass on the horizon forewarned of a flash storm.

"Really, Jon, there's not much sense in this," Maria called out to Bartlett, the wind pressing her hair against the side of her head.

"Nonsense, we'll just have to be more canny about it. It's the pond or bust. It'll be calm there." Bartlett shouted back. "Come on."

He grasped her hand and pulled her close into the cover of a dune.

"Now," he said confidentially, "are you ready to run the gauntlet?"

Maria was confused.

"We're not doing battle against the wind you know," she said.

"You never know. We might get mowed down by sand pebbles between this dune and the next. We'll have to be fast."

Before she had a chance to protest, Maria found herself being yanked into the flow of wind, Bartlett racing ahead of her, yelling at the top of his lungs.

"*AIYIIII . . .*"

When they reached the objective he dropped his hold on her hand and went charging half way up the dune still yelling, and then swung his arm as if he were hurling something onto the top of the dune. Then he slid back down the steep dune toward her, laughing crazily and then rolling into her.

"We made it," he said jubilantly, gasping for breath, "and I got 'em."

"Certainly we made it," Maria said irritatedly, and then she turned away, "and it seemed to me they got you."

"Aw come on, Maria . . ."

She turned on him. "I don't like your war games, Jon. I don't think they're fun or funny."

"OK, OK, I'm sorry, really. Maria." He turned her face around to him. "Really, I'm sorry. I won't do it again. Come on and smile . . . please."

She did, and they walked on entangled in one another's arms, over an embankment, down a sharp sandy escarpment that funneled into a small freshwater pond. Around it a necklace of cattail spikes and cusped spears of swamp grass safeguarded the still brown water.

"Finally," Maria breathed with relief as they passed out of the wind, half walking, half sliding down to the fortified edge of the pond.

"I've been thinking about these cattails all day, Jon. Do you remember how we used to rob them of their seeds?"

Bartlett nodded and then withdrew to a small clump of pine trees. It was a spot that he remembered well. Maria turned from the spot amid the sedges and watched him gravitate toward the trees. And then she turned back, reaching for the firm brown tufts of cattail spears, pulling off a clump of the tightly packed seeds, watching them expand, alive and reptilian in her hand, before they blew away, pollinating the countryside.

"It's fantastic," he heard her utter in wonderment. "Jon, can you see? It's like a small bird in my hand."

Bartlett nodded again instinctively, watching her in fascination, knowing that he would treasure this memory of her.

"Maria," he called to her finally.

The girl looked up at him sitting under the pine trees. She hesitated a moment as if pondering whether to join him, and then she called up, "OK, I'm coming."

She grabbed a last tuft, and then ran to him, flopping down by his side.

"Watch, Jon," and she opened her hand slowly as it rested on his knee, and then both watched in amazement as the myriad furry seeds pushed away from one another and gained their freedom.

"Maria," he said, reaching for her open hand and closing it gently, "you're so beautiful."

She looked up at him and then craned her head to his

cheek, kissing it and then resting it in the cradle of his neck. They lay back on the bed of pine needles, he unbuttoning the thick coat that disguised the movement of her body, his lips tracing the fine lines of her face, across her moist eyes, down her long nose to the full lips, and then to her long white neck; his hands exploring her long side, up and down, and then to her firm breasts.

"Maria, I love you."

Maria sighed and murmured his name against his cheek, her body alive now, her hands reaching for him, timidly clumsily, unsure.

"I want you," she heard him say, "I want you for my wife, I want you to have my children."

Maria seemed to shudder a bit, but grasped him tighter.

"Come," he implored her, "let's find someplace warmer."

"No, Jon, I don't want to. I can't."

"Why," he asked softly, "I want you so much."

"No, it's too fast. It's too fast."

"But it may be two years before I see you again. Please."

"No Jon. It won't mean anything. And besides . . ."

"Besides what?"

"Besides . . . You get such control over me when I give in. I don't want that, especially when you're going off."

"Come with me, Maria," his hands fumbling under her layers of clothing, soft and insistent.

Maria struggled to control her desires.

"When you come back," she whispered against his cheek, her eyes tightly closed, her mouth parted and moist against him.

"No, now," he insisted. "Come with me to Hawaii. Be my wife. We'll have children."

He pressed himself harder against her and Maria felt herself slipping away, torn between her desires and her memories and her idea that this time she must, she must resist, even if it meant . . . He was too much of a man to stop now when she said no; anyway her No did not even convince her.

Her eyes opened and she looked up into the million patterns that the pine needles and branches made against the gray shifting sky. She pulled Bartlett's flaming body against her tightly, and whispered, "Jon, I could have had a child by you last year."

"A child?" He did not understand. He raised to look into her calm face.

Maria reached a hand to his lips, tracing his fine mouth slowly.

"Yes, Jon. A child."

"But . . . you never told me."

"You were gone. You had gone off to the Army."

"But you could have reached me. You could have reached me before . . ."

"No, I was scared to."

"Scared. Why scared?"

"Because I was afraid you'd turn against me. You've always talked about things you wanted to do before we settled down. I knew you wouldn't be happy until that was out of your system. . . . And besides I didn't want to be an Army wife."

"But how could you go through . . . that . . . without help?"

"Never mind, Jon. It's not important."

"What about now, Maria? What can I do? Will you be my wife now? We could . . ."

"Don't be silly, Jon. You're less free than ever."

"But you could come to Hawaii with me. There's a good Oriental art program there and . . ."

"Stop it, Jon. You have no idea of what will happen to

you in Hawaii, or how long you will be there, or whether you'll go on to Vietnam. . . . I can't get into that with you . . ." and then for the first time there was a crack in her calm demeanor, "I've lost so much already."

Twenty-four hours later Lt. Bartlett stood in the Cleveland airport with his parents and Maria. His green uniform was pressed and professional, his garrison cap cocked rakishly to one side.

"TWA Flight 2-3-4- for Chicago and San Francisco . . . now ready at Gate 14. . . . All aboard. . . . Final Call." The husky female voice breathed sensuously between each word. No doubt she was a honey blonde with long hair, draped over a couch in a silk lounging outfit in a room somewhere above the terminal.

"I don't know why they need to have sex in airplane announcements," Bartlett's father offered to break the tension. "Well, so long, son," and he offered a firm handshake. He kissed his mother. "Good luck, dear." And then he turned to Maria.

"Goodbye, love," he said almost in a whisper, meeting her soft stare, his hand reaching to her cheek.

"Goodbye, Jon," she said.

He turned, put on a pair of wrap-around sun glasses, and walked out the door toward the plane. His mind raced ahead to his next assignment.

IV

November 28, 1966

A day later Lt. Bartlett stood in Col. Shannon's outer office on Sword Island. It seemed to the young lieutenant that he had been in a thousand offices like it, well-lit, the monotony of its green walls broken only by an uninteresting photograph of a Hawaiian coastal scene and pictures of previous commanders of the 243rd. On the door the words COMMANDING OFFICER were printed in boldface.

"Sergeant Major, this is Lieutenant Bartlett. I think you are expecting him," his escort said.

A ruddy-faced veteran named Donahue looked up from the color combat foldout from the latest *Army Digest.* From habit he slowly looked Bartlett up and down as he did with privates. Lieutenants were no different from privates to Donahue. They both had to be made into soldiers by sergeants. Bartlett handed the sergeant major a copy of his orders as civilities were exchanged.

The colonel was informed that his new man was waiting to see him. Bartlett's uneasiness grew as the minutes dragged on. Finally a voice came over the sergeant major's box.

"Send him in."

Bartlett knocked in the customary military fashion. To a gruff, clipped "come in," he opened the door. Taking more heed of his straight military walk than of the man in front of him, he stopped three feet from the desk. With a smart, unnoticed salute, eyes straight forward, he blurted out,

"Sir, Lieutenant Bartlett reports for duty."

The tall, bald man whom Bartlett approached was absorbed in a lengthy document, or at least he gave that impression. His desk was strewn with the reds and blues of classified documents. Behind him a map of the Far East with red button-lights indicated locations of the field elements. The buttons, Bartlett found out later, did not light up. The colonel's sallow face verged on old age, wrinkled under the eyes and around his small colorless lips. There was a dull sheen to the eagles on his collar, signifying a long duration in rank.

"At ease" came the command as if that were possible for the lieutenant or desired by the colonel.

"Bartlett," the colonel began, looking at his new man for the first time, "I have no control over the men who are sent to me. If I did I might be running a unit that was gathering some important information instead of this lousy collection of boneheads. I did not ask for you, and I don't particularly want you. College boys your age and with your inexperience have no business in the game. It's tough and it's cruel and there's no place for mama's boys.

"Counterintelligence has investigated you. They gave you a clearance, but I'll tell you this right now. We make the final judgment on the loyalty of our people, not some junior college punk posing as a counterintelligence agent. Nobody trusts anyone else around here, least of all new people. That's the way I like it.

"You're in a very privileged position in this Army, young man. Lots of men your age are getting their asses shot off in some stinking rice paddy in Vietnam. They're losing their buddies to a four-foot-ten runt in black pajamas who's beating them at every turn. Here you sit in the paradise of the South Seas after a measly year and a half in the service. My advice to you: remember what a good deal you got and how quick you can lose it.

"I'm sure I don't have to instruct you about who runs this unit. I'm in every corner of this operation. My eyes and ears are everywhere. I dare you to try to put something over on me, son. I'll nail you to the wall. Now, I'm running no goddamn popularity contest around here. But my people are loyal and I'll know if you step out of line."

The colonel leaned back in his chair and studied his man in silence for a moment. His voice lowered as he resumed the offensive.

"You have been brought in here for a special project. The Department of the Army thinks on paper you have the qualifications. As far as I'm concerned, your qualifications end with your languages, and you'll have to prove they're good enough. Anything else you've got you'll have to show. I'll be watching. Like I said, I had no control over your coming here, but by God, I can sure get you out in a hurry. And out means one thing—a one-way ticket to Vietnam. The planes leave from Hickam ten times a day.

"You're here to take charge of a sensitive project. Your target is southern China. We want agents blanketing the North Vietnam-China border, because when the Marines start north from the DMZ the Pentagon has to know what the Chicoms will do. Get this straight. This unit has only one mission: to support the Vietnam war in any way we can. Our existence is justified by how well we perform that task. I don't know what your feelings are about the war. I don't give a damn. You could be a goddamn hippie for all I care. But you *will* produce or you'll ship out."

The colonel again picked up the document he had been reading. Without looking at the youthful officer, he muttered, "Lieutenant Colonel Pelsey will give you a briefing on Operation Jonah. That's all."

Lt. Bartlett snapped to attention and saluted.

"Thank you, sir."

The salute was perfunctorily returned. Bartlett did an about-face and started out of the room. Just as he reached the door, he heard the colonel's voice behind him.

"Hey, George." Bartlett turned, confused as to whether the commander was talking to him. "George" was how Shannon enjoyed putting people in their place.

"Me, sir?"

"Yeah, you. Sergeant Major Donahue handles skinned knees around here, so if you have any problems of that nature, see him."

A weak "Thank you, sir" was all the lieutenant could muster.

Quite an assemblage greeted the lieutenant's emergence. The glint in the spectators' eyes betrayed their enjoyment of the situation. All had endured more or less the same, perhaps in a different vein, though inexperience, loyalty, and Vietnam might not have been quite the threats to them as to Bartlett. How rattled would the young man be, they wanted to know. It was a good insight into the man.

"Well, how did it go?" a captain inquired.

"Instructive," replied Bartlett, but he was visibly not as cool as all that.

Sgt. Maj. Donahue smiled to himself, wondering if he could have done as well.

In the weeks that followed, the lieutenant threw himself into his new project with a vigor and excitement that he had not known since college. First he read into the operations of the 243rd and everything about the Southern China provinces that was available in the unit. When he exhausted that material, he gained permission to read the pertinent Army and CISCO documents kept in various repositories throughout Hawaii. He waded through strategic target studies, insurgency and sabotage manuals, population guides. He became an expert on uranium ore production in Kwangtung Province, native tribes in Yunnan Province, tourist sites in Kwangsi Province. By using the bombing encyclopedia, he learned to interdict overland supply routes by bombing strategic targets, how to locate transformer and switching stations which if sabotaged would disrupt the social organization of hundreds of thousands of Chinese. He became expert in pinpointing dams whose destruction would stop all but token production. The phrases swam in his head: "Serious damage to equipment could result in prolonged isolations of large industrial and administration centers because of dependence on outside sources of supply for replacement parts and equipment . . . interdiction . . . food denial . . . reactive measures . . . population control . . . infrastructure . . . target acquisition."

Throughout his orientation Bartlett cleared his study through Lt. Col. John Pelsey. Pelsey found a pleasant freshness in the young man, a nice change from the regulars who handled the day-to-day work without interest or flair. He even admitted to Bartlett that he felt as if he had been working in a musty room for two years at the 243rd. Yet the hardened colonel had no illusions about his student. Experience counted in success in the military world, though Pelsey at least was willing to argue that new blood had its use. The boy was green and could be dangerous to the mission—and just as dangerous to Pelsey, whose career would be jeopardized if Bartlett slipped up. For it had been Pelsey's idea to bring in a young outsider. The chief requirement for the 243rd was to get someone situated in Kwangsi to be ready to report on the Chinese reaction to the forthcoming Marine invasion of North Vietnam. Pelsey had argued that the 243rd could not fulfill its mission with the deadweight it had. With computerized efficiency the Department of the Army had spotted Bartlett's language proficiency in Chinese and Japanese, his training in intelligence and OCS, and had ordered him to the 243rd. Col. Shannon had been right. Bartlett was indeed in a privileged position. But in allowing the plan to go through, Col. Shannon had placed responsibility for Bartlett's participation squarely on Lt. Col. Pelsey's shoulders.

Of this background Bartlett knew nothing. He perceived only Pelsey's interest in him, and he responded to it. Before they met, the tall, trim colonel had been described to Bartlett as "an officer from the tip of his head to the end of his toes," and he came up to that high praise. He had deep blue eyes that twinkled and a mouth of straight white teeth that smiled wryly when he told you that your work stank. His dark tan nearly obscured a covering of Irish freckles, and the tattoo on his right forearm (a snake coiled around a bloody sword) which he had had done in a heady moment during the Korean War was a dull blue so that one could no longer read the Latin inscription above it. His head crooked slightly forward when he walked, and Bartlett wondered if his posture had a connection with the scar on the back of his neck. Lt. Col. Pelsey was a veteran of Special Forces duty in Vietnam.

In the first month on Sword Island Pelsey put Bartlett through some tests, small probes to see if the young man was up to the mission. Was he tough enough? Was he cold enough? Three weeks after his arrival on Sword Island, Pelsey called the lieutenant over to look at North Vietnamese propaganda pictures of alleged atrocities. Flipping through the pictures, mostly of bomb damage, Pelsey came to a napalm victim. "You've seen one napalm burn, you've seen them all," he said with that smile of his and looked deeply into Bartlett's eyes for a reaction. Not seeing one, he followed up, "Of course, they're not really people anyway."

Bartlett returned a level gaze and faked a snicker. He would not be caught up by such a crude thrust as that.

A week later Pelsey called Bartlett in again. The lieutenant had been on Sword Island for a month now. It was time to see if he made the proper moves.

"Bartlett," the action officer began, "how are you enjoying the game?"

"Oh, fine, sir. It's interesting." Is this another test, Bartlett wondered.

"Good, good. There's a lot you have yet to learn and not much time to learn it. Take places we have to be careful of, for example. CISCO won't let us into Hong Kong since they have a delicate agreement with the limeys. I guess they're afraid we GIs will screw up. Of course, they're not so great themselves. Like the flap they got into trying to buy the Prime Minister of Singapore. You can buy anybody in South East Asia: the Vietnamese, the Filipinos, the Thais, the Gooks, and who did they have to try it on: the one guy in the Orient who wouldn't go for it. That incident put back years the technique of straight cash deals with government officials. Oh, well, the breaks of the game. Anyway, that's beside the point. Let's get down to specifics. What do you know about the Si Kiang River?"

"Well, sir, it's the main river of southern China. Its source is west in the mountains of Yunnan Province, it flows east through Kwangsi Province, and empties into the South China Sea near Canton and Hong Kong."

"Have you taken a special interest in it these past few weeks?"

"Yes, sir, I have."

"Why?"

"Because, sir, it is important militarily. It's the main avenue of commerce for the southern provinces. Fleets of junks and sampans carry commerce between Canton and inland cities. Except for the river there are only footpaths and a few bad roads. The river would certainly play a major support role in any Chinese invasion of North Vietnam. And if there ever were a war with China, stopping traffic on the river would immobilize Kwangsi Province."

"Do you think it has any value operationally—from our standpoint here?"

"Well, sir, naturally, if we could get a man on the Si Kiang reporting military movements along the river and down the railroad into North Vietnam we'd really have something. But I doubt that we could ever get him in there. The area surrounding Hong Kong is especially closely guarded."

"Wait a minute here, soldier. You've been talking to too many of the old hands around here. Look, Bartlett, understand one thing. There is no operation that we can't do if we plan carefully. We have enough people on this lousy island who will tell you you can't do this or that. They'll say it's too dangerous, or too insecure, or that we'll lack control. I'm tired of it. You don't know enough about this business to think negatively, so think positively, man. That's what you're here for."

Bartlett was stung by the comment. Pelsey sat back and watched the dismay come over the young officer's face. Then Bartlett's eyes lit up, and he began to speak excitedly.

"All right, sir, what about this?" The young officer began, "As far as I can gather from the files, we've pushed people out of submarines and planes into isolated places hoping they will make their way safely inland and proceed to their target. Most have been caught because people know one another in rural underpopulated areas. If somehow we could introduce a man into the riverboat business, get him established making commercial runs between Canton and Nanning, then we'd be sitting pretty."

"How do you propose to do such a thing: put a boat with our man in the belly of a whale and have him regurgitated above Canton?" Pelsey was enjoying himself.

"I'm sorry, sir, I just don't know enough about travel restrictions on the Si Kiang or the geography of the river delta to say how the problem could be solved. But if you give me a couple of days I'll come up with an answer."

"Whoa, slow down now, you're racing too far ahead. The important things is that you're thinking as you should. I think you're going to be a good gamesman, Bartlett. It's best to think of yourself that way. Skill and planning are important just as in chess, but luck is usually the final arbiter of who wins. All you can do is know your opponent's potential, study his moves, and then you take your chances."

"I was captain of the fencing team at the Ohio State, sir. Maybe some of the same principles . . ."

"That's very nice. Now, Bartlett, listen carefully. In the past six months quite a few people have been playing the game with the Si Kiang. You're right about its military importance. It's the key feature of southern China. And the key target on it is Nanning in Kwangsi Province. With a man there we could gauge not only river traffic, but, as you mentioned, traffic down the main railroad to Hanoi. OK, let's get down to business. In six months the Marines will invade North Vietnam. The big question is, how will China react? The Pentagon is looking to the 243rd, Lord help them, for the strictly military side of that question. We must have a man on target in four months."

"That's pretty quick, isn't it, sir?"

"You're damn right it is. Now then, the plan is to slip a

man in a small sampan into the traffic on the Si Kiang. His boat will look like a thousand others that travel the river. The difference will be that under the floorboards behind a tool box there will be a miniature burst transmitter. With this device our man will communicate with us.

"If you'll remember, the Si Kiang Delta, like most deltas of big rivers, is a maze of channels. Before Mao, the delta was the lair of river bandits who raided the boats of rich Canton traders. That's why if you read any books about travel along the river in the 1920s, all the boats were heavily armed. Well, there are still a few renegades in there, only today they're in the pay of CISCO.

"CISCO believes that if we can get a man to the delta, one of their bandits can guide him through the maze, past Canton, and put him on his way to Nanning. They will provide him all he needs to pass any river patrol check: identity documents, public security registration card, cargo manifests, travel permits, grain cards, and so on. Once he's on target at Nanning, he'll try hooking into the local boating cell unless he can avoid it without suspicion. We'll provide him with enough yen to buy groceries for six months. There's only one hangup at the moment, Bartlett. The man. Who will be the man to go?"

At this point the colonel paused, glanced at the lieutenant playfully and reached for a cigarette. Bartlett shifted uncomfortably in his chair. "No, that's impossible," he thought to himself. "He can't mean *ME!*"

His cigarette lit, the colonel reached to a pile of papers on his right, thumbed through to the middle of the pile, and pulled out a document with the red coversheet marked SECRET.

"Here," he said, "read this message."

The message was in teletyped caps.

SECRET. LIMITED DISTRIBUTION. PRIORITY

FROM: LANCER TAIPEI

TO: TONTO HONOLULU

SUBJECT: Y-140

1. HAVE COMPLETED ASSESSMENT OF Y-140. FAVORABLE INDICATORS: FANATICALLY ANTI-COMMUNIST. STILL SPEAKS HAKKA FLUENTLY. ROMANTIC ABOUT KWANGSI COUNTRYSIDE AND CLAIMS WOULD DO ANYTHING TO RESCUE FATHER FROM COMMUNISTS. CAPABLE STUDENT KAOHSIUNG UNIVERSITY. ASIAN PHILOSOPHY MAJOR. FINISHES NEXT MONTH. CONFUSED ABOUT FUTURE.

2. LANCER FEELS Y-140 CAN RPT CAN BE RECRUITED FOR OPERATION JONAH. HOWEVER WE FEAR UNIT DOES NOT RPT NOT HAVE PROPER PERSONNEL TO BE SUCCESSFUL. Y-140 NOT RESPONSIVE TO OLDER MEN. NO RAPPORT HAS BEEN ESTABLISHED.

3. RECOMMEND YOUNGER MAN WHO COULD POSE AS UNIVERSITY STUDENT, TOURIST, OR WRITER ATTEMPT RECRUITMENT. SHOULD BE KNOWLEDGEABLE IN ASIAN THOUGHT. DOES TONTO HAVE CANDIDATES?

4. IF TONTO LACKS ASSET LANCER WILL ATTEMPT RECRUITMENT IF INSTRUCTED. PLEASE ADVISE.

5. THIS MESSAGE HAS BEEN COORDINATED WITH CISCO.

RANDSOM

Bartlett lingered over the message. He glanced back through it, absorbing, pondering, frightened.

Finally he lifted his eyes to the expressionless visage of the colonel. His superior took a deep drag on his cigarette.

"What did you major in in college, Bartlett?"

"Philosophy, sir."

"Well, Lieutenant, what a coincidence."

TROOP INFORMATION — Block 1

MARINES BATTLE REDS NEAR DMZ, KILL 23

SAIGON (CDN)—US military officials said yesterday American bombing raids on North Vietnam will be intensified in the next two months because of Hanoi's rejection of peace feelers. They said targets will include objectives previously on the off-limits list.

"We tried to be nice and it didn't work," one US command officer said.

CASUALTIES RISE: 394 DEAD OR MISSING

SAIGON (NYT)—At the restaurant atop the Caravelle Hotel, customers clamored for window seats and then sat eating steak and lobster and watching planes and helicopters strafing the city's outskirts.

Nearby at the US Officer's Club atop the Rex Hotel, captains and majors munched hamburgers and leaned out the windows to catch a glimpse of the fighting.

When the thump of rockets drifted up to the restaurant one man tore himself away from a row of slot machines to look out over the city. After satisfying himself that the building was in no immediate danger, he returned to the slot machines.

On the streets below venders did a brisk business in black market cigarettes at 50 cents a pack.

"Dirty pictures—American girls," one vender called out in an effort to bring customers to his stall.

AIR WAR 4TH BIRTHDAY: 2 PLANES LOST

TAY NINH (NYT)—An Army captain peered out the window of a small plane on a recent trip over enemy infiltration routes between Saigon and Cambodia and said again and again, "I can't believe it—I just can't believe it."

There were bomb craters in neat clusters of destruction as far as the eye could see. The land looked like a giant piece of swiss cheese. Some areas had been hit so often that the craters blended to form scars of canyonlike proportions.

RHINOCEROSES AND ELEPHANTS ARE AMONG WAR VICTIMS

SAIGON (NYT)—Vietcong terrorists killed 3,820 civilians in 1967, more than double the 1,618 slain in the previous year, the US Mission said today. In addition the Vietcong were reported to have kidnapped 5,388 civilians compared with 3,507 in 1966.

PLEIKU SUFFERING FROM PROSPERITY:
Influx of GIs Spurs Crime, Slums, and Inflation

HUE—The young Vietnamese civilians and the soldiers of the Vietnamese last detachment that has been left at Headquarters make the Marines angry. Marines are dying and being wounded a few blocks away in one of the hardest battles of the war. It has never been more clear that they are fighting for their own pride, from their own fear, and for their buddies who have already died. No American in Hue is fighting for Vietnam, for the Vietnamese, or against Communism.

Ah know what ah'm fightin fur: fur God, the flag, and you, ma.

CASUALTIES
(Continued on pg. 39)

SAIGON (NYT)—Two South Vietnamese drivers employed by the US Embassy apparently turned traitor and helped a Vietcong commando squad invade the embassy grounds Wednesday night.

CINCPAC, 17 Apr 67: asked if the three Communist divisions in and just north of the DMZ were capable of staging a major offensive through the zone, Admiral Sharp said, "I wish they'd try it. We look forward to the opportunity of using our firepower and mobility."

CINCPAC, 11 Aug 67: Concerning the possibility of a ground invasion of North Vietnam, Admiral Sharp said, "Militarily it is always good to take the offensive action."

MY THO—The helicopter banked steeply to the right and started into its dive over the village.

"It's supposed to be the center hut," Capt. Lewert's calm voice crackled over the intercom to his machine gunner. The village sprang into life with the percussion flapping of the Huey overhead.

Lewert spotted the hut where the VC were reportedly hiding. Coolly he positioned his bird for a rocket strike. His eyes looked up from his instruments in a final check. At the door of the center hut a woman stood with a child, seemingly transfixed watching the machine bearing down on her. "HOLD YOUR FIRE!" Lewert's voice screamed over the box as the Huey started pulling out of its dive "HOLD YOUR FIRE!"

Suddenly the straw roof of the center hut was ablaze with enemy gun flashes. Lewert's legs were riddled with AK 47 bullets. Back at the tent hospital at Pleiku, the doctors decided one leg would have to come off.

V

September 11, 1967, near Kaohsiung

"I would like to spend my life here." Chuang broke the silence. "I'd build a small cottage by the brook down there as it runs into the pond. It would be nicer if I could build under the cliffs in Kuelin in Kwangsi Province, but this would do. One would get to my house only by foot. Each week I would walk to the *hsien* for groceries."

"And what would you do all day?" Bartlett asked, sitting up to look down the small incline to the spot of Chuang's imaginary house and then back to the Chinaman's skeletal face. He had never really studied Chuang's face before—his brown eyes, large for an Oriental, usually so alive and almost frightened, but in this pastoral scene relaxed for the first time; the high rounded cheek bones that sloped down to cavernous cheeks and full lips; his dark Hakka skin.

"Oh, that's no problem. I would perfect an art form. I'd paint or write poems. Perhaps I'd become a woodcraftsman. Anyway, I would aspire to become a small creature in the whole scheme. Not a master or a tyrant of nature. Just a part of it with no pretensions."

"And when will you do this, Chuang? After you make a lot of money and retire to seclusion, a wise old man?"

"I'm not sure when, Mr. Baskin. Perhaps when my family is together again. Perhaps when, as you say, I have a little money. I don't know when. But nature and beauty and art, and of course, family—these are the enduring things. It's important to realize such an obvious thing when you're young.

Then you can make the decision early to free yourself from society and pursue these lasting values."

"But what if beauty is not the most enduring quality, Chuang? What if it is ugliness? What if mechanized, even Americanized, ugliness is spreading everywhere throughout the world? Perhaps it will engulf your stream and pond and house here. If a machine doesn't do it, a nuclear bomb might. It's becoming harder and harder to escape an ugly, violent world."

"I do not want to escape it exactly, Mr. Baskin. I must know it. I want to experience it. It's the pattern of youth on this island that I want to escape. Here one is innocent and naive until twenty-nine. At thirty we are corrupt and cynical . . . I am like Eve in your lore. She is persuaded by the Devil that she must taste evil so that she might avoid it in the future. My folly will not have such vast implications for mankind as Eve's. So I will taste reality but not be consumed, caught, engulfed by it so as never to escape."

"I don't understand you, Chuang. Your family has been split by an evil political system. Your land is threatened by the same system that permits no detachment, no freedom to pursue nature or beauty or things of the spirit. How could you detach yourself from the struggle against this evil now, even if you had the means to do so?"

"You see, Mr. Baskin, I think you and I see the nobility of a human being differently. For me it is detachment from society. For you it is involvement against the evils of society. Society to me is fixed. It will not change very much in my lifetime. And, if it does, the contribution that I could make to the change would not be worth bothering about. But I do control my life. I control its direction. I control my mind and my body. I can develop them or let them degenerate. That's what's wonderful about freedom. I can hope to sharpen my senses and my mind. The wisdom of older men, the frivolity of children, the beauty of my surroundings, the ways of birds and trees and flowers—all these I can learn from. And when I die, I'll feel that I have cultivated what was given me by my ancestors as much as it was in my power to do so."

"Oh, Chuang, you talk in misty ideals when such real dangers are all around us. There's only one way that the ideal situation which you describe will be possible: that is if good men sacrifice their detachment for the benefit of others. What if when I die, I can say I added a little something to make a better world for people like Chuang? I accomplished something that was broader than my life, my family, something that was important to my community or my country. Will I, too, not have achieved a wisdom and a sense of satisfaction that's similar to yours?"

"Ah, but don't you see, Mr. Baskin, that your chances for success are so much smaller than mine? How transitory will be your achievement if you succeed; how embittered you will be if you fail. And even if you do succeed, how will you have spent your life? You will have spent it fighting ignorant, treacherous, unimaginative men. And what will happen to your ideals and your sensibilities in the process? If you succeed, it will not be because you are idealistic but because you are—how do you say—a smooth operator. Do you think it is possible, realistically, to be a smooth operator in the cause of beauty and spiritual development? One has to make a choice."

Bartlett did not like the choice. It was too close to home.

"You see, Mr. Baskin, I suspect you of being ambitious. Ambitious men who have notions of 'saving mankind' or preserving freedom are the men who get us into wars. That's what's wrong with your leaders and your country. You wish to promote your ideas of the world, not by example, but by force. In the end, you are known, not by the ideas, but by the force alone. That is all because you are ambitious. You see, I believe in the force of example. But let's not talk politics. It's so depressing these days."

For minutes, neither spoke. Bartlett lay back in the grass again, his hands locked behind his head. His face frowned slightly, in struggle with a thought. Chuang sat cross-legged, gazing out on the tranquil scene. But his mind was also absorbed in the content of their conversation. He liked the directness of this earnest American. Among his friends there was rarely discussions of values or politics. It was forbidden, for one thing, and anyway, it was rare that his friends had individual ideas.

"Do you know the writings of Lin Yu Tang?" Chuang asked.

Bartlett nodded. "Some," he replied.

"Do you remember this? 'The world has too many cold-hearted people. If sterilizations of the unfit should be carried out as a state policy, it should begin with sterilizing the morally insensible, the artistically stale, the heavy of heart, the ruthlessly successful, and all those people who have lost their sense of fun in life—rather than the insane and the victims of tuberculosis. . . . Many a prostitute lives a nobler life than a successful businessman.' "

"It's easier for you to think of sterilizing people than for me."

"Do you think it uncivilized?"

"Yes, on a mass scale, certainly."

"Ah, you are a privileged American."

"Would you like to be the judge of who is to be sterilized for being artistically stale?"

"I would prefer to handle the heavy of heart." Chuang smiled, but the comment shocked Bartlett.

"I don't think that's funny. On the mainland there's a

government in which just such a state policy is conceivable except with a petty bureaucrat as judge. I can see some value in fighting against the suffering and degradation this causes."

"Oh, Mr. Baskin, I'm not convinced that my people suffer so much more under Mao than under Chiang. The true suffering comes when families like mine are rent apart with some on the mainland and some in Taiwan."

Again there was silence. The American's thoughts turned coldly to his mission. Why should he become interested in this Chinaman's notions? He could not come to like him as a friend. Never fall in love with your agent: it was a cardinal rule of the game. Pelsey had stressed it time and again. What value did these weird Oriental thoughts have for him anyway? Look what a mess they had made of things. Bartlett did not want to think about it.

No, he must not allow himself to fall into these discussions anymore. He must get on with the job. A cynical, laughing, scoffing exterior would be his best defense. He vowed not to broach any subject again that was not directed toward recruitment, and he longed for the whole dreadful business to be over.

The two young men passed into the Canton Moon Restaurant. Bartlett had surveyed the scene the night before. The Canton Moon was situated on the edge of the city market and was run by Johnny Yung Kuo, a non-political man engaged on the side in some small-time smuggling to Hong Kong and Foochow. It was to his advantage to mind his own business.

Bartlett managed to keep a half step ahead of Chuang. He aimed for a table in the corner. From there he could watch the door. It was morning, so business would be slow. The noise from the street was sufficient to drown their conversation. If Chuang made a scene, Bartlett could swiftly leave the restaurant and be lost in the morning market crowd. He had specifically worn a drab gray jacket from a cut-rate tailor—the uniform of the petty bourgeois in the street.

"Chuang, we've talked of many things in the last few weeks: your memories of Kwangsi Province, your concern about your father, your uncertainty about the future. But your family situation interests me most of all. Have you thought about point-blank asking for permission to get him out? There must be some channels."

"I think it's impossible. There are no channels. We can't even write to him. Naturally, I've inquired. Out of the question, everyone tells me. I'm afraid, Mr. Baskin, that short of an invasion of the mainland, there's no chance of getting father out."

"Isn't there such a thing as unofficial channels?"

"I'm not sure what you mean."

"Unofficial channels. Somebody, not in the government, who might know how to get into Kwangsi with a word to your father, or even get him out."

"I have never heard of such a thing, Mr. Baskin. Have you?"

"Of course, I've read in books about the underworld of Macao or Taipei. Those stories are always romanticized, I guess. James Bond is always lurking in the darkness in some crazy disguise, after having had twelve women. Perhaps such things exist. . . . Perhaps we could find out."

Bartlett watched Chuang's eyes light up. This was the right tack.

"Also in those books are the reports of big money that changes hands. That's out of my range."

"Maybe money's not the only way, Chuang. Maybe there's something else you can offer these people, whoever they are. I'm not sure what, but it might be worth exploring.

Naturally the first question would be how much you really care about getting your father out of Kwangsi."

"I want that very much, Mr. Baskin. You know that. Ching-tsu is my flesh and blood, my father, my ancestor. I owe him very much. I wonder if you can appreciate how important that is amongst Chinese?"

"I can only sense it, I suppose."

"I know he will come." Chuang was becoming intense now, his large eyes darting back and forth from Bartlett to the other customers in the Canton Moon. "At least I think family is still more important to him than the Cultural Revolution. It's possible, I guess, that the Party has succeeded in twisting his mind. But if there were anything, anything at all that I could do, I'd try it."

"You say that, Chuang, but do you realize what that means? What you are asking is a very risky thing. People might have to jeopardize their lives to accomplish it. Put yourself in their place. Anybody would have to be pretty highly motivated to make an illegal trip six hundred miles into Communist China for your sake."

"I'm serious about it, Mr. Baskin. I'll do anything if there's a chance, even risk my own life."

"And what of your detachment that we spoke of last week, Chuang? Risking your life is not exactly pursuing the goal of that house by the pond."

"Family is the only thing that matters, Mr. Baskin, the only thing worth risking one's life for. Please don't tamper with my feelings on that. . . . Have you ever heard of anyone who could arrange my father's return to Taiwan?"

"I'm not sure, Chuang. But I have an idea. I have a friend who may be able to help you. I can't tell you who he is because it's not exactly legal, you see. I tell you what I'll do. I'll get in touch with him tonight and see what he has to say about your problem. Meet me at the Brazil Coffee and Music Restaurant tomorrow morning at eleven. Do you know it?"

"Yes. It is just off Seven Sages Road."

"That's the one. I'll tell you what he has to say then. In the meantime, Chuang, you must not tell anybody what we talked about. If you do, your chances of seeing your father will be nil. My friend is likely to help you only if you keep this a secret between you and me."

"All right, Mr. Baskin. I promise. I will keep all our talks confidential. Thank you so much, sir. You're very kind to make this sacrifice. Tomorrow at the Brazil. I won't tell anyone."

Bartlett stood up and, with a benign smile and a modest look, offered his hand. "See you tomorrow, Chuang."

The Great World Hotel was ten blocks from the Canton Moon, but the lieutenant was in no hurry to rush back. He was too frightened. Well, you've finally done it, Bartlett. You're a smooth operator now. Congratulations. How does it feel?

Scared and a little sick, Lt. Bartlett walked expressionless for six blocks, accompanied by the stench of the sluice along the sidewalk, past a national policeman in a rumpled blue uniform. The American nodded a greeting. "After all," he thought, "we're in the same game." He stopped at the display window of a sandal store. Checking in the reflection of the glass for anyone who might be following him, he walked into the store and tried on a pair of cheap thongs. Minutes later he came out with a package in his right hand and proceeded up the street two blocks. There he stepped into a pedicab. "Take me to the Spring and Autumn Pavilion," he told the tattered driver, and off they went. He was not being followed.

That evening in his hotel, spacious in the old Manchu tradition, Bartlett struggled to keep hold of himself. He dawdled over his notes. He could not concentrate on them. I must get a message off to TONTO, he kept saying to himself, but he sat with paper in front of him and besieged by a montage of clashing remembrances—a melancholia of lost beliefs and twisted values. His mind rested on the image of a stark anteroom of an Oriental doctor's office. There he sat rigid among Chinese peasants. On the door Chuang's name was printed in florid characters. He was waiting to be sterilized as one of the "heavy of heart."

Finally, he managed to flush the phantom out of his mind with the thought of Maria. She would not approve of his sterilization. With a hectic flourish of the pen, he wrote:

Subsequent interviews with Chinese umbrella salesman rewarding. Hope to wrap up final details tomorrow Baskin

He tossed the wrinkled piece of paper on the front desk and addressed the concierge. "Could you send this telegram to 'East West Enterprises, Lani Bird, Honolulu,' please?"

The thin Chinese nodded obsequiously several times, and Bartlett hurried out of the hotel.

The meeting at the Brazil the next morning would be the dangerous one, Bartlett knew that. He was tense and excited as he dressed and went down to breakfast. He would not need coffee this morning. A little cognac to calm him down would be more in order.

It was not that he cared very much whether Operation Jonah was blown or not. For Chuang's sake he almost wished it would be. But for his own sake he must be good. He must pull it off. It would be too embarrassing if Chuang yelled for the police. How humiliating to face the recriminations from the likes of Big Dean Shannon. Success was the route of least discomfort.

Lt. Bartlett was on the streets by 0800 hours. He wandered down to the market of Kaohsiung. It was teeming with activity. He stopped to talk with a group of coolies squatting in a circle plucking the feathers of duck. They were always surprised to confront a Westerner who spoke their language.

"Just in from Peking?" Bartlett asked with a glint in his eye.

A scrawny coolie looked up from his squat and displayed a fine set of rust-colored molars.

"Home grown on the Love River," he replied. Bartlett recalled what the Love River looked like and decided not to have Peking duck in Kaohsiung.

At 1030 hours Bartlett cased the area around the Brazil. The cut-rate tailor shops along the arcade were beginning to open. A sea breeze winnowed dust and debris down the littered street.

A block away from the restaurant Bartlett passed a cluster of American GIs. He nodded to them as a brother in the bond.

"What d'we do now, Hinton?" one was saying. A cap line ran across the middle of his forehead separating the weathered texture of his adolescent face from a soft whiteness above.

"Well, Jersey said the Home Sweet Home was good."

"Looks to me like all the girls are goin' t'be ugly this time of the mornin."

"I don't know. These Mona Lisas go round the clock. They know we're only here five days."

"Mona Lisas, hell. More like Whistler's muthas."

"Man, you got no room to complain. I told you to sign that contract back there."

"Fifteen bucks for that pig. I've seen better at An Khe for a quarter. I'd rather spend my money on a damn Buddha statue."

"Lose your horns at An Khe then. I don't care."

Bartlett watched them sidle down the street. Back home

they'd be swinging a chain on the block, he thought to himself. Here like lost sheep they roam the squalid subculture of the Orient and wait for their lousy five days to be over.

At 1045 hours Bartlett entered a magazine stall across the street, eight doors down from the Brazil. He stationed himself in front of the stall window, looking out onto the street, and began to flip through a Chinese girlie magazine. The Oriental girls did not really make it in this format, Bartlett decided. Their breasts were too small, and they did not taper enough at the waist. Perhaps if the girls could come alive on the page, look up at the reader with an elusive, sidelong glance, and swirl their long black hair fan-like, then . . .

1055. Bartlett kept glancing up from his magazine to the street. A minute later Chuang came into view. He was wearing a white short-sleeved shirt and carried several books. The street was not crowded. A young woman in bare feet with pants rolled up slopped water onto the street several doors down from the Brazil. Chuang walked into the restaurant. Bartlett kept his eye on the street for another minute.

Suddenly, a shrill voice behind him made Bartlett jump.

"GI on leave?" He turned to see a wizened old woman smiling up at him. He nodded. "Have more pictures behind counter. You like see?"

"No, thanks," muttered the American, "I have enough already," and walked out of the stall.

Chuang had taken a table in the back corner of the Brazil. "Good move, agent," the lieutenant thought as he walked toward him.

The Oriental rose to greet Bartlett as he approached the table.

"Good morning, Mr. Baskin. Good morning," cheerily.

"Hello, Chuang," Bartlett replied quietly, "you're looking well this morning."

"If I do, it's a miracle. I didn't sleep so well last night. Look, I've brought you a present. It's a novel by Lin Yu Tang. It's not his best, but perhaps after reading it, you'll understand better what I was saying at the pond."

"Chuang, how kind of you. Does it describe your future life of leisure?"

"Perhaps it will describe yours, Mr. Baskin. You may be converted."

A round-faced waitress appeared suddenly at the table. Bartlett ordered coffee for two and looked at Chuang's expectant face. Beethoven's "Pastorale" played on the stereo system. Bartlett waited in silence for the coffee to be brought.

"Chuang, my friend does not think he can help you."

Chuang's face dropped.

"Your problem is just too difficult. Getting into Communist China is difficult enough anywhere, much less Kwangsi. That would take a lot of money and a lot of men. And what can you offer in return?"

Chuang said nothing. He took his cup in both hands and slowly raised it to his lips. Suddenly at the door there was a shuffling of feet and Chuang glanced around to see a Nationalist major walk in and take a seat several tables away. The young Chinaman looked nervously back at Bartlett, and Bartlett decided to press the advantage.

"He sees only one possibility, Chuang, and I hesitate to even mention it to you." His tone was quiet and unemotional now.

"What is it, Mr. Baskin? Please tell me," Chuang whispered.

"The possibility is for you to go in yourself. You know the country. He knows how to get you in safely and how to get you out with your father. But there would be one condition: that you must stay six months. He can arrange for you to do that. He's a professional. He knows exactly what to do because he has done it successfully many times before. In that six months you'd have to do several small tasks for him. In ten months you'd be back with your father and have a considerable stipend to boot."

Chuang was silent. He took a long draft on his coffee again and looked up at Bartlett as if he were disappointed in him.

VI

October 2, 1967

The train finally rolled into Taipei. Bartlett was swept out onto the platform by the same screeching throng and further out of the station exit. Above the din a voice quacked departure times over the loudspeaker. The young man aimed for a niche in the outside wall of the prewar, Japanese-built station, where he might escape the surge. It was a good practice in any riot. Safely there he brushed off his clothes and waited for the press to spend itself. He had been told to expect a battle, but this was something else.

As the crowd thinned, Bartlett took out a blue handkerchief from his back pocket and wiped his brow, replacing it in his left coat pocket. Then he waited. In thirty seconds or so he noticed a disheveled Chinaman approaching, a wrinkled yellow cap atop his thick black hair.

"Saa, you Grand Hotel?" in coolie English.

"No, I'm going to the China Hotel."

"China Hotel very easy find. I take you there. Very cheap price."

"How much?"

"Eight NT."

They went off together and piled into a beat-up Datsun minicab. After several blocks, the driver turned his head to the American in the back seat and said, "Welcome to Taipei, Mr. Bartlett. I hope the train trip was not too unpleasant."

"The trip from New York to Washington is more comfortable I admit, but not quite as colorful. You are . . . ?"

"Captain Fung."

"Ah yes, captain. I've seen your reports. Do you make the trip often?"

"Quite frequently, yes sir. You see, my parents live in Tsing Yao, a suburb of Kaohsiung. My father is quite ill, and I go down regularly. I'm used to the crush, of course, and sometimes I even take the tourist train."

"I see. What's the schedule for today?"

"I'll take you to your hotel now. We have a room for you in a small pension in the hills above the smog line. It's clean and spacious. We know the owner well. At 1600 you're to call Maj. Randsom at this number. You'll be having dinner with him at his house. Col. Kuo, the commander of SMITE, and I will dine with you also. I'm scheduled to take over Y-140, you see."

"Very good. I think you'll find him very pleasant."

"Oh, I feel as if I know him very well already. May I congratulate you on your work, sir."

"Thank you, Captain."

"Oh, and I brought you an afternoon paper."

Bartlett opened the *China News* and glanced at the lead story.

MAINLAND FOLKS ANXIOUSLY
AWAITING COUNTERATTACK

Taipei—An ex-Red cadre who recently defected to Free China told a Taipei press conference yesterday that farmers and workers on the mainland have been longing for an early counterattack from Taiwan under President Chiang's leadership. "Everyone hates the regime over there," he said. "They are anxiously awaiting a chance to revolt." On Oct. 10 this year many fishermen went out in their boats to pick up floating copies of President Chiang's "Double Tenth Message," he said. These messages are floated to the mainland by offshore defenders.

For the next few days Lt. Bartlett lapsed into a consuming torpor. He had asked not to begin with Y-140 until he had a chance to unwind a bit. His request was granted immediately. The young man, after all, was a celebrity. He had pulled off a difficult recruitment. Bartlett languished by the pool in the American compound and read a book on flower arrangement. He took long walks, "meaningful walks" a friend called them, through the mountain parks of Taipei. And there was a splendid display of Sung scrolls at the National Palace Museum. Bartlett marveled at the delicate precision of one series which depicted life at a Sung lord's mansion in each month of the lunar calendar.

Lt. Bartlett had hoped for a sensuous deliverance from the tension of his mission in these few days, but his mind seemed to lock mechanically into reflection on what was happening to him. This was, he concluded, a last stage, a final act, a disappointing denouement: his last hours of innocence. This Circe called reality had petted and fondled and caressed him until now there was no escape, no turning back from the final inexorable deflowering. It was as if he had sold himself to some giant grotesque whorehouse, and had found that whoring wasn't so bad after all.

Three days later Bartlett assumed once again the efficient businesslike veneer that military men inspired in him. In his more relaxed moments he liked dealing with these soldiers. Their direct looks, their straightforwardness, their habit of constantly judging appearance made a man stand up and cope with the problem at hand without whimpering or stuttering. Once that could be done, handling them was a breeze. And one was occasionally surprised to find beneath the facade a dose of soft-hearted sentimentality.

But in Maj. Stocky Randsom, Col. Shannon's detachment commander in Taiwan, there was little difference between the military man and the real man. As both he was dull and ineffectual. A good-natured, rotund officer with the face of a pharmacist and a peculiar bouncy walk, he inspired neither loyalty nor contempt in his men. He was just there—not much of a threat. His favorite joke was to ascribe all his problems to the "generation gap." A penetration boat would not arrive on time—it was the generation gap. A good officer would be transferred out—up would go the thick hands; it was the generation gap.

Randsom rested his military career on three claims: administrative ability, twenty-one years of loyal service, and no black marks. It is difficult to know where else he might have rested it, surely not on imagination or aggressiveness. Like Shannon, he too was maddeningly close to a promotion. If he made lieutenant colonel, his life, he felt, would be a success, and then it would be on to a comfortable retirement in Coeur d'Alene, Idaho.

Because Shannon held an important sway in Randsom's promotion chances, Randsom lived in perpetual terror of his superior. It was a state of mind, however, which had kept him out of trouble with previous commanders. So he valued the things in Taiwan that Shannon valued in Hawaii. He kept the lawn immaculately clipped. His men spent weeks before a Shannon visit repainting signs and walls, planting flowers, and otherwise adorning the small building. It was said that if the night before a Shannon visit, an enlisted man threw lime on the lawn to turn it yellow, Randsom would have a heart attack the next morning.

Even though Randsom had occasioned it, Lt. Bartlett's arrival in Taiwan was greeted by the aging major with reserve and suspicion. He had not really expected Shannon to find anyone capable of recruiting Y-140, but now that Bartlett had not only been found but had pulled off the job, Randsom felt uncomfortable in the extreme. He consoled himself by berating Bartlett's unorthodox military appearance. Shannon had sensed the command difficulty from a distance, and sought to assuage his detachment commander's feelings in a message. In it he promised the lieutenant's stay in Taiwan would be temporary.

But the mission had acquired a life of its own beyond Randsom's feelings now. Two months had passed since Lt. Col. Pelsey had given Bartlett his mission. Y-140 had been recruited, and the Marines were readying their invasion plans for North Vietnam. Between Randsom, Kuo, Fung, and Bartlett, it was agreed that Y-140 had to be launched in seven weeks. Military necessity demanded it.

By choice and by ability, Maj. Randsom handled the logistical side of Operation Jonah and left the personal side to Bartlett. In the first few weeks of working together the arrangement worked fine. SMITE handled the acquisition of the sampan. CISCO came through with the Chinese Communist documents for a river boatman. Their man in Macao established contact with a guide in the Si Kiang Delta. Luckily the Cultural Revolution had not yet spoiled Macao as an espionage trading post.

There would, of course, be no weapons. Weapons get you into trouble, Pelsey had said. Any agent who has to use a gun is dead already, at least to US interests. Unless the agent is in immediate danger of his life he shouldn't carry them. The key word was immediate. He's always in danger of his life. That's part of the game.

Immediately after Y-140's recruitment, he was moved into

a SMITE safehouse on the outskirts of Kaohsiung. The speed of the move allowed no time for second thoughts, and Bartlett's plan was for training to begin as soon as the agent had been briefed on security. The house, a low-slung wooden structure with a thatched roof, was located off a dusty road not far from the Love River, and might have passed for a functionary's suburban home. SMITE maintained a few ducks and chickens in the yard as a final touch. Inside, the house was comfortable in a Chinese fashion, but what lay beyond the visitor's view gave the structure its distinctive character. The living room where Capt. Fung would conduct the training was wired for sound and organized for filming. The upstairs contained equipment that provided instant communications to SMITE headquarters and to the local police box. A room next to the living room was outfitted for monitoring the training proceedings without being noticed. In the next seven weeks Y-140 was to lead a much more public life than he realized. From his vantage he would come to know only Fung, who rarely left him; and an old woman who did the cooking and was actually a major in SMITE; and an 18-year-old houseboy, a SMITE lieutenant.

Lt. Bartlett spent the first two weeks of training in Kaohsiung planning the agent's training schedule, watching Capt. Fung's technique, relaying every significant detail to Maj. Randsom in Taipei. Fung and Y-140 moved immediately into a disciplined schedule:

5:30—Awake
6:00—Run two miles
7:10—Breakfast
8:00—General background on the New China
10:00—Calisthenics
11:00—Responsibilities of a commune member
12:00—Lunch

1:00—Language class with the houseboy in Hakka and Cantonese
2:00—Boat handling and fishing techniques
4:00—Memorizing Mao's quotations
5:00—Leisure time, games, three-man volleyball
6:00—Dinner
7:00—Reading, games, meditation

During the Hakka dialect classes, Capt. Fung slipped away for a daily conference with Bartlett. Bartlett would criticize Fung's performance of the previous day on the basis of the tapes and films. He would give new instructions on any pertinent information from Randsom.

Bartlett worked out the overall training schedule during his time in Kaohsiung. The agent would receive his final briefing on the way to the target, but he had to command the skills of radio communications, common fishing techniques, and the latest Cantonese and Hakka speech patterns first.

He had to be grounded in the latest political events between the Liuist and the Maoists in Kwangtung and Kwangsi Provinces, so that if he were spotted by either group he would know how to act. It would be a laborious, time-consuming process. But after the first week when under Bartlett's guidance Fung broke down the agent's innocence and reserve toward the new knowledge and, indeed, succeeded in firing his imagination about the upcoming adventure, the training began to go well. At the end of the second week Bartlett returned to Taipei, encouraged by Capt. Fung's efficiency and Y-140's alertness.

From Taipei Bartlett steadily took over effective control of the whole operation. He demanded from Fung an evaluation of each training session, in addition to the tapes and films. He chided SMITE for their slowness in outfitting the sampan with its electronic devices. When CISCO came in with only fragmentary data on river controls in China, Bartlett demanded more: What patrols would there be on the Si Kiang? Would they understand Y-140's dialect? What would be his problems on target? Go to Washington if need be, but get the information. This operation would take advantage of every knowledgeable source there was.

It was at the beginning of week four that the crisis occurred.

Bartlett had been at work early, mulling over a halfway-to-launch report for TONTO on Y-140's training. Randsom broke his train of thought at 0930 hours.

"Message from the jolly green giant," he said and threw the perforated message on Bartlett's desk.

TO: LANCER, TAIPEI
FROM: TONTO, HONOLULU
SECRET. LIMDIS. TOP PRIORITY
SECURITY BRANCH FEELS AFTER READING FUNG OPERATIONAL REPORTS AND BARTLETT EVALUATIONS THAT EXISTENCE OF AGENT FATHER IN NANNING STILL UNVERIFIED. SUGGEST YOU ADMINISTER SODIUM PENTATHAL UNDER TIGHTLY CONTROLLED CIRCUMSTANCES TO DETERMINE FATHER'S EXISTENCE AND VERIFY STRONG AGENT MOTIVATION FOR RESCUING FATHER FROM MAINLAND. SHANNON

Lt. Bartlett read the message twice and threw it on his desk. For a moment he did not speak.

"He can't be serious," he managed finally, looking at Randsom. "It must be a joke."

"It's no joke, Lieutenant. There's nothing funny about this operation."

"But the agent is no goddamn pin cushion. You just can't administer a truth serum to this man without destroying the trust that Fung has built up."

"How do you know there's trust there? How do you know we're not just being made patsies of?"

"Because I know. I know better than anybody. I know Chuang has his father in there. He's willing to risk his life to get him out."

"That's not enough for Shannon or security. I'd calm down and get a little professional."

"Professionalism . . . you and your professionalism, sir. It's just goddamn barbaric to stick a needle with that stuff in somebody's arm and then let him spill out his whole life. Anyway, the doctors say it's not reliable. It's not needed, and you jeopardize the whole operation."

"Barbaric, eh? You better watch your step, Lieutenant. You're coming very close to court-martial behavior. Whether it's needed or barbaric, as you say, doesn't matter. It's ordered. And I'll have my written orders for you within the hour. You will supervise its administration and the questioning."

Randsom turned away and started out of the room. Then he turned back to Bartlett.

"Oh, and Bartlett, you may just have gotten yourself into a barbaric business."

Stocky Randsom kept his word. Bartlett's orders to Kaohsiung with the purpose of the trip clearly stated were before him within the hour. Randsom informed him that a Navy plane had been layed on to take him to Kaohsiung in three hours. Bartlett was instructed to have a list of questions for Y-140 within an hour, and at 1300 to report to Randsom for a briefing. After his briefing the lieutenant was to pack a bag and be at the airport at 1400 hours. Meanwhile Randsom would handle the serum, getting it to the airport, and reporting the lieutenant's arrival to SMITE, Kaohsiung. There was no time for reflection. Bartlett did as he was told, and found himself two hours later standing beside a Navy two-engine S-2-F ("stoof" as the flyers called it), handing his bag up to a Navy lieutenant, accepting a small metal box from Randsom, saluting him without a word, and climbing aboard the small plane. He wondered later if Randsom's last look had meant, "So long, chump." Actually the major was thinking about the generation gap.

Lt. Bartlett made his way to the small compartment behind the two pilots, placed the small metal box on the seat beside him, and strapped on his parachute.

"You can just keep it loosely fastened, Lieutenant," one of the pilots shouted back to him over the roar of the starting motors.

"Right, sir." Bartlett yelled back, and then he settled into the narrow seat amid the wires and dials and tried to make himself comfortable.

The noisy plane rattled down the runway and finally lifted off—with such an air of crisis in the cockpit that Bartlett wondered how these men stood the anxiety so often. But the small plane soon labored gamely above the clouds. Only the snow-capped peaks of Chungyang Shanmo rose above the pristine whiteness in glorious purity, and Bartlett abandoned himself to his thoughts.

If only his parents could see him now! His stark, Calvinist father, his delicate artistic mother—they had been ideal parents. They had been strict with him when he was young, and he approved of that now that he was old enough to see its value. They had taught him to be disciplined, to respect rules, to keep an orderly mind and orderly surroundings. His education in a church school was to strengthen these bounds of moral behavior, and to provide the content for the mind and the spirit.

It had not been the formula for nourishing a brilliant mind

or an artistic sense but rather for cultivating a solid citizen, well-educated, right thinking, not prone to prejudices or easy answers or fashionable foppery. He had not done poorly by these privileges.

His parents had been against his induction. They could be idealistic about duty to one's country in the abstract. His father had joked, "When you raise that right hand and step across the line, son, raise three fingers to signify three years out of your life."

His mother could not be so jocular. When he did not tell her what he was learning in intelligence training, she got the notion that he was grooming to parachute into North Vietnam. Once he was in, his father had tried to put the best face on it. He gave his son essays about duty and war. One of them was William James's "Moral Equivalent of War."

"Have a look at this, son."

The text had read, "We must make new energies and hardihoods continue the manliness to which the military mind so faithfully clings. Martial values must be the enduring cement: intrepidity, contempt of softness, surrender of private interest, obedience to command . . ." And yet Bartlett had seen only the veneer of these virtues in his service, and behind the facade, the opposite qualities: flabbiness, self-serving, deceitful, cowering before vain, unreasoning, and often racist command. Was this the enduring cement that James wanted for American society?

All the schooling, all the love and tendering, all the happiness of the home, all the nurturing of the tender instincts had been a preparation for this experience: the systematic denial of it all: training to lie, training to kill, training to use people and then discard them. What was its purpose? To defend his country, to defend its values, to destroy an alien system across an ocean. But which values were being destroyed in the process? Who was being destroyed? If his parents could only see him now.

"Hey, Lieutenant, want a cup of coffee?" A face framed in a helmet was shouting at him.

Bartlett nodded.

"It's in that steel container with the black button in front of ya."

Bartlett nodded his thanks.

Suppose Chuang was a double? Bartlett smiled to himself as he filled a cup with coffee. Perhaps I'm not so smart after all, he thought. What a twist if he, rather than Chuang, was being duped. Yet he did not expect that to be the case. Chuang was the most sensitive, the most thoughtful, the purest person he had met in years. He was above deceit.

And yet if it were true, should he think any less of Chuang? Perhaps Chuang had deep beliefs that motivated him. No, he, Jonathan Bartlett, was a worse double. He was acting efficiently, consciously, conscientiously, directly against his beliefs. Why? For the excitement of it. That was the truth. He didn't have the courage of his convictions. He had substituted a fool's notion of courage, a counterfeit courage. He wouldn't be like those softies back home, he boasted to himself. He was a he-man, testing his manhood by fire. Big deal. "You asked for this, baby. It was what you wanted." That was why he had slapped Maria when she called him a coward, he realized for the first time. He had thought of himself as being so brave to go in.

The truth serum—why had he found the idea so abhorrent? Was it really so barbaric with Chuang? Bartlett looked down at the small metal box on the seat beside him. Truth in a little metal refrigerated box. He could not lie to it. Using the serum was no more barbaric than the rest of the operation. It was the idea of that needle going into *his* arm that he could not tolerate. The sensation, as he closed his eyes, of watching all his defenses crumble almost beautifully. "Now tell me, Lieutenant Bartlett," he could hear Col. Shannon saying firmly, "Is your heart in this operation?" "No." "Will you carry it through?" "Yes." And then Maria floated by. "Are you for peace, my love?" "Yes, everyone's for peace, until you get a chance to participate in war."

There could be no doubt when the small plane began to descend. Nothing whispers or glides or soft-cushions on a S-2-F ride. But in case his passenger was something of a vegetable, a pilot yelled back, "We're going in, Lieutenant. Better fasten up."

Bartlett looked out over the dull red rooftops and chaotic roads below. Exciting Kaohsiung, dust capital of the world. He reached over and put his hand on the metal box.

The brain, that sublime manipulator of human thought, emotion, and action, operates in three stages: receiving a stimulus, integrating that stimulus into knowledge, and initiating some action in response. Its powers of integration, the psychiatrists will tell you, are infinitely complex, and often operate at their most complex when a human promotes a fiction either on himself or on others. In other words, fiction is more difficult for the human brain than fact.

It was Chuang's complex mental process, his level of integration, that Shannon and his instrument, Bartlett, proposed to slow down with truth serum. The drug would simply make it too difficult for Chuang's brain to disguise the truth through inhibition or defense or analysis of the questioner's intent. His brain would not be operating fast enough. Bartlett's mission was to supervise the injection of the sedative, to do the questioning, and finally to administer a heavy dose of the drug that would put the agent out for the night, and block or muddy his memory of the conversation.

On the following morning Lt. Bartlett was up at 0400 hours. He held a two-hour briefing with Capt. Fung at the SMITE installation near the safehouse. It was decided that the drug would be administered at 1900 hours that night, so that the agent would sleep through the night when the questioning was over and wake up on his regular schedule the following morning. Y-140 was informed at breakfast that the evening would contain a physical checkup and a few shots. A SMITE doctor was instructed on the administration and monitoring of the drug. The human body quickly metabolizes pentathal, so to keep the subject in that useful midstream between consciousness and unconsciousness, the drug must be constantly injected.

Y-140 was cheerful that morning. He informed Capt. Fung that he had had a fine night's sleep and had dreamed of the cliffs of Kuelin.

"That's fine, Brother Chuang," Fung said, "Perhaps you would like to paint this afternoon after we read from Mao."

Y-140 was delighted. Fung promised to get the materials.

Lt. Bartlett spent a busy day of conferences with SMITE on details of the launch, and then at 1530, a half hour before Y-140 and Capt. Fung returned from the boats, he slipped into the safehouse, and made himself comfortable in the concealed room adjoining the living room. He was interested to watch the agent's session on Mao.

Y-140 and Capt. Fung burst back into the house precisely on schedule, flushed and joking after two hours on the water. Fung shouted to the old woman in the kitchen to bring them some tea, and then they got right down to Mao's quotations.

Bartlett was impressed with how easily the two men worked together, and how seriously they took their tasks. They seemed to have a genuine friendship and respect for one another. Only once in the hour did the seriousness break, and then only for a second.

The agent was parroting a quotation as he had been taught: "The atom bomb is a paper tiger that the US reactionaries use to scare people. It looks terrible, but in fact it isn't. Of course, the atom bomb is a weapon of mass slaughter, but the outcome of a war is decided by the people, not by one or two new types of weapons."

He finished and then he giggled a little.

"Have you ever seen a paper tiger, Brother Fung?"

Fung shook his head.

"Perhaps the President should disguise one of his bombs in a huge paper tiger. It could be an Oriental Trojan Horse. I'm sure Chairman Mao would be impressed by the paper pop."

They both giggled a little and then went quickly back to work.

After the class Chuang sat by the window, charcoal and ricepaper before him on the desk. Bartlett watched with fascination as the Chinaman's hand moved delicately over the paper. Often Chuang would stare out the window for some time before making a stroke, his eyes following the games of the scrawny chickens in the yard. His dinner was brought to him at the window as he requested, and the old woman inquired if he wanted another pillow to be more comfortable. Chuang refused without seeming to have heard the question.

At 1850 hours there was a slight knock on the door. Fung answered it, and admitted a Dr. Hu Shih, who entered the living room and bowed perfunctorily to Y-140. Officiously he opened his bag and began to spread out a few things. Y-140 was asked to come to the couch. The doctor tested his pulse and listened to his heartbeat. He did some thumping on Y-140's back and chest. He looked down his throat and into his ears. Then he instructed the agent to lie down on his back. The doctor took out a syringe, broke the sterile glass covering around the needle, and then slowly filled the receptacle with thirty ccs. of liquid.

"Be brave," Fung joked. Chuang smiled.

The doctor dabbed the patient's antecubital vein on his inner arm and then injected the needle into the main line. Slowly he depressed the plunger, and in five seconds of cerebral deceleration, the agent was delirious.

Capt. Fung excitedly beckoned to the blank wall, and Lt. Bartlett emerged. He took a seat on the opposite side of the couch from Dr. Shih and looked down at the subject. The slim Chinaman's eyes flickered open and shut. Beads of sweat formed on his high forehead.

"Brother Chuang," Bartlett began, "can you hear me?"

"Yes," came the slow reply.

"Brother Chuang, this is James Baskins."

"Ah, Mr. Baskins. . . . I wondered where you were. You didn't write."

"No, Chuang, I wasn't sure where you were."

"We never had enough time to talk, Mr. Baskins."

"That's true. Perhaps someday when we are both not so busy."

"Yes. I hope so."

"Now that you are so close to seeing your father again you must be very happy."

"Yes."

"Where is your father now, Brother Chuang?"

"In . . . Kuelin."

"Not in Nanning."

"Or in Nanning. . . . I'm not sure."

Chuang's speech was slow, thick-tongued.

"What was the last news you had of him?"

"Five years ago . . . when he was released."

"Released?"

"Yes. He had been . . . in jail for ten years."

Chuang's head began to move from one side to another. Bartlett glanced at Dr. Shih. The doctor administered another half cc. of pentathal and Chuang relaxed.

"What was his crime?"

"He had organized . . . the escape of Kuomingtang . . . from Kwangsi Province in 1948."

"Brother Chuang, do you have a deep feeling for your father?"

"I . . . I . . . hardly know him."

"But . . ."

"I was only . . . nine when I saw him last."

"But why do you take risks to get him out now?"

"I must . . . I must get him out. It is my duty."

His head was moving again. He tried to rise up off the couch.

"Hold him down, Fung," Bartlett shot the command.

"The escape . . . the escape . . . things were happening so fast . . . gunfire . . ."

"What about the escape, Chuang? There is gunfire outside. People are frantic . . . Your mother . . . Your father . . . What happened Chuang? Try to think."

"Pack your things, my son . . . Where are we going? . . . Away. . . . But what about father . . . What about father . . . He will have to stay now. . . ."

"You were talking with your mother."

"Yes."

"Why did he have to stay?"

Chuang writhed again, this time tears began to roll down his sunken cheeks. Dr. Shih plunged another half cc. into his vein.

"Why did your father have to stay, Brother Chuang?"

"Because . . . because I had told . . . I had told them."

"What had you told?"

"I had told them where he was. I had told the Communists where he was hiding. . . . But I did not know. . . . I did not understand. Hui Yang had instructed me. . . ."

"Who's Hui Yang?"

"Neighbor Yang did not tell me it was the Communists. . . . He said they were patriots. . . ."

"Why would Yang do that?"

Chuang was trembling with sobs now.

"It was his deal to get many of our area out. . . . I did not know. . . . I was too young. . . . But I did it. . . . I sacrificed my father. . . . They would never have found him otherwise. . . ."

His words began to trail off.

"Pack your bags, my son. . . . He will have to stay now. . . ."

Lt. Bartlett looked at Capt. Fung, and then to Dr. Shih.

"OK, doc, slug him," he said.

The emotionless doctor nodded and then slowly forced the remaining twenty-five ccs. of pentathal into Chuang's arm. He was out within a second.

At 2300 hours that night Lt. Bartlett arrived back in Taipei. He was met at the plane by Maj. Randsom and Col. Kuo, the commander of SMITE. Bartlett handed over the tape of the interrogation and the empty refrigerated box. He was driven to his pension, and collapsed in exhaustion on his bed without undressing.

At 1030 hours the following morning he reported to Randsom. The commander greeted him with a broad smile.

"Hey, Bartlett, how lucky can we be, eh!"

Bartlett did not reply.

"Good work, Lieutenant. Really. I'm going to write you a letter for it."

Bartlett nodded without taking much notice, and then said, "Look here, Major, are you sure that last slug will make him forget the conversation?"

"Pretty sure. He could have a kind of dreamy recollection of it, but that's all. He'd never be sure it took place. Relax, my boy. Don't sweat that."

Bartlett seemed unsatisfied.

"Course, we could have used puromycin," Randsom followed.

"Puromycin?"

"Yea, they use it to block memory in rats. But I was afraid he might forget all that other stuff we taught him as well."

VII

November 8, 1967

In the next two weeks Lt. Jonathan Bartlett adopted an icy coldness toward Maj. Randsom and others in the detachment. The young officer kept after his commander with endless questions about the final plan, no longer framing them in his customary friendly manner. But the major had had so many unsuccessful operations that he viewed this one with dull bureaucratic indifference. This infuriated Bartlett. Y-140 was not a number. He was a human being. The man's life was at stake. Didn't Randsom understand that? Only Chuang's safety mattered now.

Bartlett prodded and cajoled the major. He stressed that the accomplishment of the mission would help both their careers and that it could only be done with thorough planning and hard work. He thought Randsom would understand that language. When he did not, Bartlett resorted to ridicule, making sure to attach a "sir" to the end of any biting comment.

"This operation is not foredoomed by the goddamn generation gap, sir," he said one time.

Only once did he get a reaction. After a period of Bartlett's insistence on some detail or other, Randsom puffed himself up and said, "Look, Lieutenant, I should know how to do it. I've been in this business a lot longer than you have."

"That's not necessarily a virtue," Bartlett quipped and walked away.

It was to no avail in the end the onus would fall on Bartlett alone.

Once in this period Capt. Fung came to Taipei for a day of conferences. During the time of checking and rechecking details, Fung admitted having overlooked an item on the fishermen's commune solidarity in Nanning. Bartlett fumed in silence, staring at the collection of maps and draft plans on his desk. Slowly, he raised his eyes to the young Chinese captain.

"If this were a Soviet operation," he whispered, his clear green eyes penetrating beyond the wide stare of the Chinaman, "I'd have you shot for that."

Later that evening Bartlett remembered the incident with a shock of disbelief. So this was how the organization got you, he thought. You start to talk their language and pretty soon you're shooting people. Maria had charged him with that very thing in their last rendezvous.

He called Fung at his family's chaotic, one-room dwelling, asked the captain to meet him at the Mona Lisa Club, and there apologized profusely.

November 20. The telegram from TONTO left no doubts:

SECRET. TOP PRIORITY.

VIETNAM SITUATION REQUIRES EARLIER PENETRATION DATE FOR Y-140. COMMENCE PHASE IV IMMEDIATELY. FROM REPORTS BARTLETT SEEMS BEST MAN FOR FINAL BRIEFING. SHANNON

"Well, the invasion date has been moved up." Maj. Randsom phlegmatically addressed his subordinate. "How do we stand?"

"Well, sir, I think he's ready anyway. We could use a little time for radio training and on Chicom fishing techniques, but I think he'll be all right without it. I guess we'd never feel he's had enough grilling. SMITE has the sampan in good shape finally. The box has been prepared, and the whole thing can be put together and loaded on the sub in a matter of hours."

"OK, let's get on with it," Randsom said around the butt of a cigar. "We'll go to Kaohsiung tonight. I'll lay on a Navy plane. We launch at 1900 tomorrow night. Twix Fung that our ETA in Kaohsiung will be 2130 tonight. And have him indicate to Y-140 that launch is imminent. That way it won't take him by surprise."

"Right, sir. Now what about the briefing?"

"You will be the only Caucasian that Y-140 is to have contact with. Check Fung's plan for bringing the agent into the Navy compound very carefully. You'll start your briefing at 1800 hours Wednesday, nine hours before we're on target. Insertion will be at 0215 Thursday. I'll check with the Navy on the weather. How secure do you think the Navy end of this has been?"

"Oh, they've been very professional, Major. They love this kind of mission, you know. It gives 'em a chance to use all that training. No, I don't think there's been any leak there. No Chinese have been in contact with the building of the box. And all the Americans knew were the specifications. We're pretty safe there."

"OK, I'll handle the Navy and SMITE liaisons if you'll instruct Fung. Make sure Fung stocks the sub with Y-140's favorite meal. He's entitled to that much before launch."

"Right, sir."

"Oh, and Bartlett, slip some beer and cigars aboard, will you? You never know, we might have cause for a celebration."

Dear Jon,

You asked me how my tour in Vietnam was in your last letter. In one word: delightful. Hue is wonderful, so calm, so enchanting and, not unimportantly, full of the most beautiful women you have ever laid your eyes on. We are in an old stucco villa built by a French rubber trader in the old colonial days. The back lawn rolls down to the River of Perfumes. The Citadel where I often go on dates with girls from the University of Hue is just across the Bridge of the Golden Waters. The old fortress is interesting both historically and militarily. I sometimes read lying on one of the ornate 19th-century cannons. The Officers Club is also within walking distance, and they often have good entertainment. Last week Martha Raye. When I get a chance, I go to the beach at Thuan An. Things could be worse.

For me, the best part is that I am finally involved in meaningful work. No more papermilling, no more Shannons, this unit does something. It's a pleasant change. Infiltration from the North is up, as you've probably read in the papers. We do our best to keep track of it and provide as many targets for the 52s and Phantoms as we can. I have about 20 assets under my control (mainly low level stuff like trail watching), and monthly dispense about $10,000.

Some predict that Hue will be a VC target soon. I don't believe it. My boys don't tell me that. We seem so removed from the war and there are so many Allied troops around. How can we lose? We have the only Vietnamese Division in Hue that the Yankee brass thinks is worth anything.

Take care. Ray

At 1600 hours the following day, Tuesday, all preparations had been made. Lt. Bartlett was driven to his quarters for a shave and a shower. He gathered a few things together: his toothbrush and razor, two shirts and a change of underwear. Bartlett smiled at his practicality. The world could crash around him in ruin and devastation, but he would remember his toothbrush.

At 1810 Bartlett arrived at an obscure, heavily guarded corner of the Naval base at Kaohsiung. Documents were presented. The driver continued on past two more checkpoints and finally arrived at a barnlike structure on the water. Except that the structure was painted flesh-color, it resembled an elongated New England boathouse. He was met there by Fung.

"He's already aboard the PT boat, sir. We blindfolded him

on the way over and on board as you told us. He did not mind after I explained that it was for his own benefit. He's a nice chap, you know."

"Fine, Fung. Who's he seen aside from you?"

"Several crew members on board. None of them are in uniform, and all are Oriental."

"Good, I'm going on board the sub. Let's see, it's 1815 now. Is that what you have?"

"Yes."

"OK. You're scheduled to depart in the PT boat in thirty minutes. We pull out in the sub in forty-five. Rendezvous at sea is scheduled for 2025. Do we check?"

Fung nodded his head.

"See you then."

At the door to the barn the impeccable officer of the day, a slim, tawny-haired ensign from Kansas with a Forty-Five strapped to his belt, recognized Bartlett immediately.

"Go right on board, Lieutenant. Major Randsom is waiting for you." A tone in the ensign's voice and the look in his eyes betrayed his admiration for his important contemporary. It did not escape Bartlett.

The slat-board passage along the submarine was dimly lit by forty-watt, red-tint bulbs. Bartlett could not make out the silhouette of the submarine, but he could feel its presence. Port water lapped softly against its hull. Bartlett walked cautiously along the passage, straining his weak eyes, afraid someone might have inadvertently left a tool box in his way that he might trip over. Across the gangway, through another security check by the petty officer on watch, awkwardly down the shiny aluminum hatch-chute. Bartlett jumped the last two steps of the ladder into the florescent brilliance of the Central Office of Control. Maj. Randsom stood amid the dials and wheels with his hands on his hips.

At 1900 sharp the doors of the barn opened and Fast Attack Submarine 242 slipped out of the harbor into the black night. The sea was calm and the sky starless: perfect conditions operationally.

The rendezvous at sea with PT-190 was flawless. Blindfolded, Y-140 was transferred and guided down the rear hatch into the after-room. The room had been modified for the agent's comfort. A straw tatami mat had been placed next to a leather couch. Bartlett had seen to it that the labels on the capstan engine overhead and on the reel of floating line at the rear of the room were changed from English to Japanese.

The plan called for the sub to stay on the surface through most of the night to make the full twenty-four knots per hour. As the glow of dawn became visible, they would dive to periscope depth. The Navy estimated that the drag of the box would slow underwater speed by five knots to seven knots per hour. If all went well, they would be on target at exactly 0218 the following night.

Maj. Randsom and Lt. Bartlett played cribbage in the compact but comfortable officer's lounge. Countless games went by and neither man spoke much. They did not have much to say to one another. Fung came in periodically to give a report on Y-140's state of mind. He was nervous, the Nationalist officer reported, but said little about it. Occasionally the agent and Fung had exchanged innocuous words. At 2305—twenty-seven hours before launch—Fung reported that Y-140 had gone to sleep after twenty minutes of meditation.

The cribbage game was broken off at that point. Randsom rolled into the narrow bunk across from the lounge. Bartlett climbed into the one above. The paint had begun to crack on the metal plating above the lieutenant's head; his tired eyes traced the crooked lines a thousand times as if it were an imaginary road map to Nanning. The submarine pitched slowly back and forth with eternal regularity as it moved over the dark sea.

Bartlett blamed his sleeplessness on the motion. He felt hot and enclosed. This is the final miniaturization, he thought, the final punishment—incarceration in the womb of a submarine. Maria. What pain she must have endured. Wizened old woman, dirty hands, back country roads, elaborate explanations, fabrications—an operation not unlike Operation Jonah. It was disgusting. And Maria had endured it all alone. How strong she was. And she bore him no grudge. And he—what could be his penance? How could he repay her? He could not replace the child. It strengthened his desire to have her as his wife. They would have ten babies in rapid succession, and the mob would blot out her loss.

And now this—this womb, this embryo of his. Maria. Bartlett's head started to swim. His child. His creation. His agent. He was writhing, perspiring, his head moved from side to side, his eyes opening to the map of Nanning above him. His birth. His abortion. . . . He must get out. He must stop it. Escape. How? The hatch in the conning tower. Negative. It was used only in desperate situations. The torpedo tubes. Out. He must get out.

Bartlett leapt from his bunk and started down the narrow passage, moving swiftly, almost running. *OUT*. Through a hatch door—he clanged it shut. Before him a long corridor. He started to run. *ESCAPE.*

Then suddenly there was a white form in front of him. A bleary-eyed sailor emerged from the latrine, doing up his pants. Too late! *CRASH!* They both sprawled headlong onto the steel slates, stunned.

It was a moment before either understood where they were. Then Bartlett shook his head, and barked, "Goddamn it, sailor. Watch where you're going next time!"

And then he slowly picked himself up and turned in the direction from whence he had come, moving painfully, rubbing his shoulder, drained, it seemed, of every ounce of energy he possessed.

The sailor watched him go, disbelieving and still sprawled in the corridor.

"Stupid grunt officer," he mumbled, shaking his head. "It ought to be against the law to let 'em on board."

The hours dragged on. Bartlett dozed. When he awoke, the undulating had stopped. He slipped on his trousers and brushed his teeth and then went up to the Central Office of Control.

"How're we doing, Commander?" Bartlett asked the burly, moustached officer of the deck.

"No problem, Lieutenant. We put her under an hour ago. It's dawn now. We're just about on the level of Swatow."

"What about the box?"

"The drag is just about what we estimated. We're making seven-point-one knots now. I think we'll be able to sustain that."

"Fine. You serve breakfast on this tub this early?"

"A cook's always on hand, Lieutenant. This is the Navy, my boy."

"I almost forgot. Thank you, sir."

Bartlett got the report from Fung that Y-140 was still asleep, and then went for breakfast.

November 22. At 1600 hours Bartlett made his way to the after-room to begin the serious business of the final briefing. With a steady hand, he put the key into the hatch-door lock, turned it, and pulled the steel door open. Chuang looked up from the tatami mat where he sat cross-legged.

"Mr. Baskin!" Chuang whispered the words with shock and suspicion.

"Hello, Chuang," Bartlett replied in a tone that one might use to greet a friend hospitalized after an accident.

"Mr. Baskin, what are *you* doing here?"

"Well, I persuaded my friend to let me come along. In fact, Chuang, I will admit to you that I occasionally work for him."

"Just who is this friend of yours?" Chuang's voice began to take on a hardness.

"I tried to explain to you, Chuang, that it was in everybody's interest, yours most of all, that you not know that."

"That's not quite good enough any more. I want to know who all this equipment belongs to."

"I cannot tell you."

"It is the Americans, isn't it? I should have known it. I am going to Nanning for the Americans, aren't I?"

"No, Chuang."

"It's the Americans," Chuang was beginning to get hysterical. "I know it. How else could you be here, and all this equipment be here. It's the American CIA!"

"No, Chuang, believe me, it's not the CIA."

"How could I have been so stupid? And how can I believe anything you say? You've tricked me, Mr. Baskin—if that truly is your name. You've tricked me."

"No, Chuang, you're wrong. Let me explain. Please, Chuang, calm down."

"I will not go to Nanning for the CIA. I refuse to go. I will not do it." Chuang's wan frame shuddered with fright.

"All right, Chuang, *NOW BE QUIET FOR A SECOND!*" Bartlett was shouting at Chuang, and shaking him by the shoulders. "*BE QUIET AND I'LL EXPLAIN THE SITUATION TO YOU!*"

Bartlett let go of him, and the agent slumped down onto the straw mat, trembling. Bartlett did not speak for a moment, and eyed the agent sternly. Then the lieutenant began slowly in a near whisper.

"It's not good for you or for us that you know this, Chuang. It's dangerous because it spoils your concentration on the tasks ahead. You must have total concentration. You must. But I'll tell you some of what is happening, and even for that I'll be in deep trouble if someone finds out.

"No, Brother Chuang, it's not the CIA. But they are involved. And you should be glad they are. They are vital to you. No one could be more expert at getting you in and out again safely. Without them you'd never have been this close to your father."

"Who is it then?"

"Your country's Army and mine."

"And so you are a military officer."

"Yes, Chuang."

"Perhaps it doesn't matter. I suspected that some time ago."

"I thought you had."

"And what do they want from me?"

"They want to know if the Chinese will invade North Vietnam."

"And if they do?"

"Oh, Chuang, if they do . . . how should I know . . . the world will be at war instead of just the U.S. and North Vietnam. . . . I can't think in these terms anymore. I can only think of your safety and your success."

"But you deceive me. How can I believe your good intentions? You've played a monstrous trick on me."

"But I did not know, Chuang. I could never have imagined that I would involve a person like you. I've been drawn into this whole scheme just as you have. But you'll make it, Chuang.

I know you will. You're the best prepared person who has even attempted such a task. I've seen to that. You have the best equipment. You have the language, and all the background knowledge. You'll do it with ease. And when you come back with your father, I'll help you build that house by the pond with my own hands."

"Mr. Baskin, you're a dreamer."

"I'm also a believer, Brother Chuang, and I pray for your success."

"Funny . . . this is the first time I remember you calling me Brother Chuang . . . except . . . except . . ."

"Except when, Brother Chuang?"

"Nothing. I guess it's my imagination again. But, Mr. Baskin, I must tell you that I would have gone ahead with my trip anyway—despite my suspicions. But now that you are here, and that you have been truthful with me, I go with a lighter head."

Bartlett looked at Chuang in silence, not knowing what to say. And then to conquer his embarrassment and his love, he switched into his businesslike, military pitch.

"Now Chuang, let's get down to specifics. I have the privilege of giving you your final orientation before the journey. Do you feel yourself well-prepared?"

"Since I don't know yet exactly how you plan to get me to Nanning, I'm not sure how well prepared I am."

Bartlett was still not sure where the agent stood.

"OK, let me see if I can show you how each aspect of your training has had a specific reason behind it. I think in the next few hours you'll see how it all fits together. Now this is how we plan to get you into Nanning and out with your father in six months."

Thus began a six-hour briefing. As time proceeded, the walls of the compact lounge became covered with detailed maps of Southern China. Y-140 would be launched two miles off the Hsi Chu Estuary of the Si Kiang Delta. One-half mile into the estuary he would rendezvous with the CISCO guide. The sampan would bear cremated remains, ostensibly those of Chuang's deceased father. Proper documents would show that he had been given permission in Macao to return the remains of his father to their homeland in Kwangsi Province. Once through the delta and into the main channel of the Si Kiang, the agent would drop his guide and proceed alone. The guide would be in the same spot exactly six months later at midnight to pilot the sampan out again. If the agent did not show, the guide would return at midnight on the first, third, and sixth weeks thereafter.

In the first three hours Lt. Bartlett went over and over the details of the infiltration. He quizzed the agent to make sure he was absorbing them. He acted the part of the river patrol, shouted at Chuang, tried to catch him up in inconsistencies. Chuang passed, but perhaps too well. He answered a little bit too intelligently, too quickly. He was supposed to be an unschooled fisherman after all.

And so they went over it again. Chuang gave less this time. Sometimes he gave stupid replies, sometimes incomplete answers. Then Fung was brought in to act the part of the commune representative. Together they read from the little red book of Mao's quotations. Fung was impressed with how well Chuang had learned his lesson. Bartlett was not satisfied, but he never would be.

At 1900 hours they broke for a meal of bird's-nest soup, lobster and cashews in oyster sauce, and green tea. Chuang talked excitedly now about his mission.

"You have planned well, Mr. Baskin."

At 2000 the briefing resumed. "On target" was the title of this portion. As soon as Chuang arrived in Nanning he was to go to his father's house in the early evening. He was to be extremely cautious about that first meeting, making sure that his father was alone and that he did not cry out upon seeing Chuang after such a long absence. Nanning maintained a 2200 hour curfew. Chuang was not to violate that. He was to discuss with his father the chances of tying into the local fishing commune. If this father could ease this entry through friends, that was fine. If not, Chuang must himself approach the local commune leader, explain that he had returned from Canton by boat after five years of military service, present his military discharge papers, and express a desire to join the commune.

After two weeks he was expected to commence his communication of military information. From that time on, every Friday at 2000 Nanning time he was to be on the air with a burst of intelligence information. He was to be particularly alert to heavy military traffic passing over the bridges of Nanning going south: unusual massing of troops in the area, rumors of an impending invasion of Vietnam, tightening of economic controls—all this Y-140 was to transmit in great detail.

Chuang was again tested and retested. He was flashed pictures of a military train crossing a bridge, and told to formulate a radio message about it. Fung and Bartlett mocked a discussion of controls and military build-up, and Chuang wrote a message about it. He was good. Fung had trained him well.

Bartlett complimented Chuang on his performance. Chuang had to be confident. This was vital to his survival. Bartlett talked to Chuang like a combat sergeant in Vietnam whipping his men up for Charlie. He must whip them up. Aggressiveness was the best way to survive, they told you.

At 2400 hours a call came over the intercom in Japanese for "Baskin" to come topside.

"OK, Bartlett," Randsom said, a discernible tremor in his speech, "we're twenty miles from the delta. Hong Kong is ten miles due west. We'll be on target in forty-five minutes."

"What's the matter, sir? Relax. You've done this many times before, remember?"

Randsom ignored the comment with a scowl.

"How's the weather?" he asked.

"Perfect. It's cloudy with patches of fog. The sea is calm. Slight wind north by northwest five knots."

"Does radar register anything?"

"It's too early to tell. Nothing out here."

"I hope we don't happen onto a limey destroyer. The British haven't been told about this mission."

"I'm sure they'll think it beastly of us if they do find out."

The sonar bleeped its eerie sounds in the background. A skinny seaman at the instrument panel intoned his readings to the commander above on the bridge.

"Depth: two fathoms. Speed: Six-point-nine knots. Radar negative."

"Right, Bartlett," said Randsom, "we'll surface in thirty minutes. The sailors have practiced this for two weeks. They can have the sampan ready to go in three minutes. We'll be on the surface a maximum of six minutes. Go back down and get Y-140 ready."

Bartlett made his way through the narrow passages to the after-room. Chuang looked up at the lieutenant as he entered the cabin. His eyes were round and dilated.

"Mr. Baskin," he said in a high-pitched Mandarin, "I'm dreadfully frightened."

VIII

November 23, 1967

> *. . . but even their ideals are perfectly good in the abstract. When you come to think of it, patriotism, order and tradition are not to be despised, are they? It's violence that makes them false and detestable.*
>
> —IGNAZIO SILONE,
>
> The Fox and the Camellias

"Position, mark, 22° 37′ 14″ N, 113° 45′ 23″ E. . . . Engine into silent running. . . . Two degrees right turn."

The commands from the captain came in spurts as if he had difficulty in formulating his thoughts into speech. He had everything under control—the figure of the modern commander alone on the bridge surrounded by a panorama of complex dials and knobs.

"Major Randsom, how are you fixed?" came the question over the intercom to the Central Office of Control.

"All set here, Captain."

"Officer of the Deck, is your deck crew ready to execute launch?"

"Roger, sir, all ready," came the clipped reply.

"OK, we surface in five minutes. No Navy personnel will utter a word unless addressed by a superior. I want to be up there no more than five minutes. Diving officer, five-degree angle of ascent."

Bartlett looked up at the clock. 0228 hours. His eyes returned expressionless to the spot on the steel slat by his foot. He had nothing to say to Chuang now. What would he say when he put the youth aboard the sampan in a few minutes? "Good luck, old chap. Have a good bash in Nanning. See you in six months," and a slap on the back? Hardly. He did not expect to see Chuang again. He had done his job now—and pretty well too. What had Pelsey said? "In the end luck is usually the final arbiter of who wins." Good luck, old boy.

"Ready in the after-room?" came the Japanese words.

"*Shitaku.*"

"Prepare to exit."

Bartlett looked across the table to Capt. Fung and then to Chuang, dressed in the black pajama pants and white jumper of a southern-China riverboatman; his face was ashen, his eyes fixed straight ahead. Bartlett motioned to them to follow him to the bench beneath the aft hatch. The three sat down in a row to wait two minutes. Bartlett watched the second hands on his watch.

China. Vast and forbidden China. Not three kilometers from the point in the sea above the submarine lay its misty coastline. How Bartlett wished that he could see it for himself. Where would he go? Peking? Canton? To the cliffs of the Yangtse or the vast wastelands of Sinkiang? No, he would probably be drawn first to Kwangsi, to Kuelin where the mountains that have inspired Sung artists lay.

But what of its government? The brutality, the robot organizations, the mass psychology. He would certainly not like to live there. He was a petty bourgeois, to be sure, and rather enjoyed being one. And yet was there a land more unique in the world? Their vision of civilization and the future was totally different from America's, and that alone was worth something. Perhaps in decades or centuries their view would produce a greater civilization. It was conceivable. They had had more experience. Perhaps it was just as well that they disallowed the intrusion of American commericalism. It certainly had not ennobled the other Oriental countries Bartlett had seen.

How could one come to hate China? The idea of a man hating a foreign country was unfathomable. By what psychological process did one arrive at such an absurd state of mind? And yet, the facts were clear. Americans looked joyously upon the Chinese cultural revolution as the beginning of chaos in China. The Chinese undoubtedly hoped our urban riots were the beginning of the dissolution of American society. What harm had China done to us? What harm had we done . . .

"Thirty seconds to surface. Depth: thirty feet . . . twenty-five feet . . . twenty feet."

There was no sensation of rising.

"Ten feet . . . surface . . . OK, Baskin, open your hatch."

Bartlett leapt onto the ladder. The wheel dog turned smoothly and Bartlett pushed up on the heavy hatch door. It swung open easily. Above there was another hatch. Bartlett scrambled up and began the same process with it. It too swung open with oiled ease, and the lieutenant emerged onto the wet boards of the submarine deck.

Already the dark forms of sailors swarmed over the deck. In the thick mist, ten men pulled ferociously on heavy steel lines that battened down a black box, perhaps twenty-five feet long and twelve feet wide, to the deck of the submarine. In thirty seconds the lines were off. Several men gave a yank on the handles which protruded from the top of the box. The top slid toward them on ball bearings. It was lifted noiselessly to the far end of the deck and there secured. Now men on the four corners unfastened the hasps that ran down the corners like the snaps on an old-fashioned shoe. They moved quickly but without panic. The sides were lowered and fastened to the gently undulating deck. The whole process had taken two and a half minutes.

Still the contents of the curious box were concealed beneath a black plastic covering. A husky seaman who appeared to be the leader of the team produced a two-foot bowie knife. Briskly he walked along the length of the dark amorphous shape, cutting along a white line painted on the plastic covering. At the end he looked up to his men and nodded. With a sharp tug, the plastic slipped to the deck. Naked, exposed in the night, lay the fruit of all their efforts—a weather-beaten, well-used, Chinese river sampan.

"OK, Chuang," Bartlett barked down the hatch as the sailors scurried for another hatch. The Chinaman clambered up the hatch ladder onto the deck. He jumped into the sampan. Bartlett turned to the conning tower and gave a quick wave. Then he turned back for only a second to Chuang. Their eyes met. Bartlett reached out, his hand reaching to the side of the Chinaman's cold neck. And then the American was gone, down the hatch, struggling with the round steel doors, and then dropping like a bundle of laundry onto the bench below.

Above there was a faint metallic sound as the sides of the box slapped against the hull. The submarine was submerging. Only Chuang and the sampan would stay on the surface.

Y-140 had been given explicit instructions on how he was to communicate with the submarine. His radio, fitted into a can of hearts-of-palm, would give off a bleep every half hour. This would indicate the sampan's position to the sub. But if an emergency arose, Chuang was to communicate directly by voice transmission to the submarine.

Not that this meant anything. If Chuang got into an

emergency, it was his ass, and no one else could do anything about it. Nonetheless, the system was considered an important part of building up Y-140's confidence in the omnipotence of the organization he worked for.

Bartlett joined Maj. Randsom and Capt. Fung in the officer's lounge. A navigation map draped over the sides of a small table in the middle of the room.

"He should be in the delta in forty-five minutes," said Randsom, and then added, "If he makes it that far, he'll be our biggest success in years."

Forty-five minutes, thought Bartlett, the length of a lecture in college or the first act of a play or one's attention span while listening to a baseball game on the radio, as late as you can properly be to a cocktail party, not nearly time enough to make love to a beautiful woman. And Chuang, poor Chuang, had chosen this forty-five minutes to put his life on the line. For what? For his Oriental faithfulness to his father? Was that possible? Is any loyalty worth dying for?

A skinny sailor stuck his head in the lounge. "Radar report. Subject position 22° 37′ 13″ N by 113°45′ 04″ E."

Randsom searched for the point amid the smattering of depth readings peppered off the land mass on the navigation map.

"Right about here," he muttered slowly, pointing meticulously with the compass. "That puts him one kilometer west of the first mark point."

Perhaps Chuang was not thinking about the danger at all. Perhaps he really was thinking that in a matter of days he would be embracing his father, telling him the grand news of their impending escape, and about the wonderful Mr. Baskin who had arranged it all. Was Chuang in ecstacy or in misery? Bartlett hoped not misery. The fear of disaster is always worse than the disaster itself. Once the catastrophe struck, the agony of uncertainty was finally over, and you could start adjusting to the devastation.

Of course, Bartlett had never been remotely involved in danger to the degree that Chuang now was. He never would be either. How foolish to risk one's life for an idea. Ideas were so changeable, so fickle and ephemeral. Act on one idea, and a while later you might be convinced that the idea was wrong, or not as important as another idea, or confused by new facts. And then what value would the action have?

No, Bartlett would not fall into Chuang's trap. The ones who took the risks never got the credit anyway. If Chuang were successful, Shannon would be thinking of ways to keep him quiet. His reports from China would be offered up to the generals in the Pentagon on clean white paper, sanitized and homogenized, like an inspected quart of milk, with all the unsavory impurities removed.

"Excuse me, sir," an excited seaman looked into the room, "we're getting a message over the auxiliary."

Randsom and Bartlett burst out of their chairs and brushed past the seaman. In the auxiliary radio room, a radioman strained to hear the message. The tape recorder was running in case he did not get it all. Random and Bartlett pushed several unecessary sailors aside to get next to the wide-eyed radioman. On the board planks outside more feet hustled toward the cramped, airless room.

A head popped in the door.

"Sir, radar has picked up a reading on a vessel closing fast on subject's position."

The radioman stopped his writing. He threw a frightened glance at Bartlett. His left hand pressed hard against the earphone.

"Well, what's happening, damnit," shouted Randsom at the radioman.

"I think we've had a break in communications, sir," afraid he might be blamed for it.

"Fung," Randsom shouted, "rewind the goddamn tape and translate that message for us."

Capt. Fung moved quickly to the machine. Chuang's singsong Mandarin crackled through the static. Fung tensely began the translation.

"High powered engine about . . . one thousand meters away . . . coming this way . . . if I can make it three hundred more meters . . . will be into shore . . . searchlight turned on . . . situation desperate . . ."

"*MY GOD, CHUANG DON'T PANIC. JUST SIT THERE,*" Bartlett heard himself shouting.

The eyes of everyone in the compartment turned on him.

IX

November 24, 1967

The submarine lay on the ocean floor in total silence for the remainder of the night. Then as dawn broke it was cautiously put into silent running and moved close into the shore of the forbidden continent, the commander constantly checking the radar for that chilling flash on the screen of the night before. With safety precautions checked and rechecked, and all men at their battle stations, the submarine gently surfaced near the spot of Y-140's last transmission.

Lt. Bartlett and three seamen climbed out on the deck, staying close to the hatch in case the sub had to submerge quickly.

One thousand meters due south of the last radio contact, the arc of the sampan bow bobbed in the ragged chop of the sea. More debris was scattered about as if by the hand of some almighty junkman. More or less in the middle of it all a sailor spotted a white jacket. Chuang's.

He was decapitated. Twenty feet away an arm floated absurdly by itself, shot off by what Bartlett estimated in his damages report a day later as a fifty-caliber machine gun.

In a broadcast monitored in Tokyo, Radio Peking claimed that the Red Chinese Navy sank a Nationalist warship off the coast of Kwangtung Province. The broadcast was received as follows:

> On the morning of November 24 a naval fleet of the Chinese People's Liberation Army sank a U.S.-made warship which was

carrying out harassment in the Southeast China Sea near Towshan in Kwangtung Province. It goes without saying that the Chiang gang's dangerous harassment and sabotage against the mainland is instigated by U.S. imperialism. The victory is a result of the extensive efforts made by the officers and men of the People's Liberation Army to raise high the great red banner of Mao Tse-tung's ideology, to attach first importance to political work, and to continuously heighten the level of their class consciousness.

The eastern coastal area of Kwangtung Province has been in a joyous mood since hearing the news of the victory. Hundreds of workers, peasants, students, and fishermen carried streamers and beat drums and gongs. When the navy men arrived, the crowd rushed forward to shake their hands and present them with bouquets.

The United States Consulate in Hong Kong issued a routine denial of U.S. involvement.

TOKYO

January, 1968

Surely it would be possible to distinguish a hierarchy of commitments. . . . Are not some commitments in a way essentially conditional, so that I cannot unconditionalize them except by making a presumption which is in itself impermissible, for example, a commitment which depends on a literary or political opinion? It is clear on the one hand that I cannot guarantee that my opinion (on Victor Hugo or socialism) will remain unchanged; and on the other hand, it would be quite ridiculous to commit myself to a future course of action in conformity with an opinion which may cease to be mine.

—GABRIEL MARCEL, Being and Having

TROOP INFORMATION—Block 2

AMBUSH PROCEDURE

Questioner: "Did you hurt your back in Vietnam?"

No. 2: "Certainly he did. He's one of the most decorated men in this unit."

Questioner: "What division were you with?"

No. 1: "Ninth Division."

Questioner: "Was it on one of their big sweeps that you got hit?"

No. 1: "No, it was a night ambush patrol in the delta. . . ."

> The ambush force is composed of an assault element and a security element. The assault element captures or destroys the enemy. It is composed of the ambush commander; the killing group whose mission is to kill or capture the enemy within predesignated sectors of fire of the established killing zone; the search party from the killing group whose mission it is to search the dead and wounded for documents and pick up weapons, ammunition, and equipment; and the front and rear stop groups who prevent the enemy from escaping through the front and rear of the killing zone.

No. 1: "We ran into about two hundred of 'em one night. There were only twenty-three of us. They wiped us out, man."

> The terrain at the site should serve to funnel the enemy into the killing zone. The entire killing zone is covered by fire so that dead space that would allow the enemy to organize resistance is avoided. Whenever possible firing should be through a screen or foliage.

Questioner: "What was the situation?"

No. 1: "Well, in the delta, ya know, there's miles 'n miles of rice paddies. Occasionally, you got a tree line. We were in one tree line. They was in another tree line across the paddy."

> The ambush element commander determines when to open fire. In close terrain, this may be on sight; in open terrain, it may be on a predetermined signal or when the enemy has reached a predetermined point. In any case the accurate, rapid commencement of fire is essential to success.

Questioner: "How were you formed?"

No. 1: "In a circle about ten feet apart."

Questioner: "Did you have any help?"

No. 1: "Ah, hell, yeah. We had gunships and artillery the whole time. There was so much shit flying you wouldn't believe it. We lay out there six hours before we got reinforced."

> Sectors of fire into the ambushed enemy are predesignated to ensure that the entire enemy element is covered by fire. Enfilade fire is desirable. The enemy is allowed no avenue of escape once he is trapped.

No. 2: "Twenty-three against two hundred's not too good odds."

No. 1: "They didn't know how many of us there was. It's a good thing they didn't know what shape we was in—else they'd of human-waved us."

> If the ambushed enemy force is a vehicular element. . . .

No. 1: "We didn't do so bad though. . . ."

> . . . initial fire is delivered against the front or rear vehicle, whichever is at the weakest point of the ambush site.

No. 1: "They counted fifty bodies when it was over and we figured they drug off another fifty."

> If both the front and rear are equally strong, fire is delivered against the trail vehicle first.

Questioner: "How many of your patrol got out?"

No. 1: "Two. It was a sorry sight, I tell you. The shit was still flying when they carried me out."

> After the ambush, the assault element moves rapidly to the rallying point covered and followed by the security element.

X

Lt. Jonathan Bartlett, 0846575, had been reassigned to a forward detachment of the 243rd in Japan a week after the Chuang disaster. There he was placed in an unimportant slot on the fringe of the detachment's operational activities. He became the fiscal officer for all cigarettes, whiskey, and girls that were offered as incentives to China-bound agents.

This reassignment had been the personal decision of Col. Shannon, whose instinct told him that Bartlett had become involved emotionally with Y-140, a temptation that everyone in the game knew as a cardinal sin. Since the operation had been Bartlett's first, the shock might have been particularly acute, and so Shannon transferred the young lieutenant to Japan with explicit instructions to the detachment commander to watch closely for any disaffection or emotional instability. By the rare twist of Shannon's mind, this detachment commander was soon to be Lt. Col. John Pelsey. It was Shannon's peculiar method of punishment.

Once in his new duty station Lt. Bartlett appeared perfectly normal. He accepted his job with enthusiasm and handled its duties with serious efficiency. Lt. Col. Pelsey watched him pursue his interest in Japanese culture and was amused by his preference for Kyoto temples over the Officers Club. Bartlett beamed a broad smile whenever his fellow officers ribbed him about it. After three months of this behavior Pelsey requested of TONTO that Bartlett be transferred back to sensitive operations.

Pelsey's decision was not precipitate. Not only had he observed Bartlett's conduct in Japan carefully but he had gone back to the files of Operation Jonah and studied them in thorough detail. He came away feeling that Bartlett had done a superb job of planning and execution—probably the best in his memory in the Orient. His recruitment of Y-140 had been a masterpiece of manipulation; his research into the problems Y-140 might have faced en route to Nanning had been meticulous; his attention to training and his professional handling of Chuang's threat to withdraw just before launch had been outstanding. These factors gained for Bartlett Pelsey's professional admiration. The operation had been exploded by that one fatal flaw that was so hard for any officer to discover or eliminate—panic under pressure. Pelsey made a note to write TONTO a memo on how agents might better be tested for this disastrous quality.

Two weeks after Pelsey's request, he received his reply in a message.

REQUEST RE BARTLETT APPROVED. PROCEED WITH CAUTION. I DO NOT RPT NOT TRUST HIM. SHANNON

Several hours after Pelsey read the message he called Bartlett in.

"Come in, Jon." Pelsey said graciously. "Have a seat."

"Thank you, sir."

"Jon, I have made two requests concerning you recently."

"Yes, sir." Bartlett's reply registered faint curiosity.

"I have requested that you become operational now that you're acquainted with Japan somewhat. I would have liked you to know more about the country and about how we function here. It's different from Taiwan. But there's no time. Pentagon requirements are stacking up on us, and as you know, we're short on operational personnel."

"Yes, sir, I'm aware of that."

"Colonel Shannon approved the request today. He will be sending a warrant officer from Hawaii shortly to take over your slot in fiscal."

"I see, sir. I think a good warrant officer could handle those duties all right."

"Now, Jon, before you proceed, I want you to know one thing. I've studied very carefully the whole file on Operation Jonah. I think you did the best job of pulling off a difficult and important operation in my memory in intelligence. You're now a thoroughly professional and highly imaginative intelligence officer, and I hope you will consider making this your career."

"Thank you, sir. I'm not sure about the career, but I appreciate your confidence."

"That bears on my second request to TONTO. I've put in your papers for promotion to captain."

"Thank you, sir."

"Now, Jon, you've had a few months to watch missions here. What do you think of this operation?"

"Well, sir, it's obviously more sophisticated than Taiwan. We were playing for bigger stakes with Operation Jonah than the missions here. But maybe these operations won't fall as hard either."

"Now, Jon, I want you to answer me honestly. Are you ready to become active again?"

"Yes, sir."

"All right. That's what I wanted to hear and it's good enough for me. Now this is what I have in mind. Last week we got in a Department of Army requirement about a group that's encouraging our sailors in port and our GIs on leave to defect. They are also involved in some attacks on

American military posts in Japan. The requirement is to determine their strength, effectiveness, personnel, and backing. . ."

When the briefing was over an hour later and Bartlett had left his office, Lt. Col. Pelsey lit a cigarette and leaned back in his chair. Bartlett was a different officer now, he thought. There was certainly not the enthusiasm that there had been in those early days in Hawaii when the young man was so fresh. Was that due to the professionalism that Bartlett had gained in Jonah, or was it something else? Pelsey's system of alarms—refined by years of judging men's strengths and weaknesses—was alerted. Yet the colonel felt that he was handling the situation properly. It was true that there was a Department of Army requirement on KAKUMARU group. But it had a low priority. If Bartlett passed, Pelsey felt he would be justified in moving him into something important.

Dear Jon,

The picture on the front of the postcard is the tomb of the Emperor Ming Mang which is six clicks south of us on the river. It's supposed to be an excellent example of early 19th-century Vietnamese architecture, built between two lotus-covered lakes. Problem is the VC will ambush you if you go by jeep, so I'm working on a helicopter pilot to fly me in.

You would have enjoyed last evening. There was a full moon, and Tra Nhon and I were out on the river on a sampan. That's the romantic thing to do in Hue. The sampans are stocked with everything a man might need for the occasion. A real mind blower.

Have a sampan and Tra Nhon reserved for the festivities at Tet two months from now. Supposed to be quite a show.

Heard you were in Japan through the grapevine. Great. See you on R & R.

Ray

In the week that followed this conference with Pelsey, Lt. Bartlett also wondered about his responses. Why had he accepted a return to activism so automatically? What was it about these military situations that elicited such motor responses? His reaction to Pelsey's straight question had come without hesitation, without the slightest flicker of doubt, and yet it was so inconsistent with all that he had been going through since Chuang's death.

For ever since his reassignment to Japan Bartlett had been struggling with the questions of his past behind his military facade. He looked upon the petty problems of vouchers and contracts as welcome relief from the obsession with Chuang's death. For when his mind was not besieged at the office with financial figures and file keeping, it drifted inexorably to the war and his involvement in it. And so he would travel to Kyoto or to a temple garden he had found in Asakusa, and there see in the grotesque carvings, the fearsome statues, not their purpose of scaring away evil spirits, as the ancients had intended, but a kind of supernatural harassment.

No one else charged him with a crime; Bartlett knew that. There was only admiration for his "professional" handling of Chuang. He had acted under military orders, and yet . . . had he not taken them one step further? Was there such a crime as acting *with relish* under military orders? Bartlett knew these inquiries could destroy him. He had read once that "the hardest sentences are those which people inflict on themselves for imaginary sins."

And yet no relief seemed to come. Some diabolical force seemed to compel him to explore the details of being solely responsible for the decapitation of a man he could have loved —in support of a war he did not believe in, for an ill-defined national interest and a campaign of anti-Communism which he felt demeaned his country, with a mission against China that might have provoked her into the war, and in collaboration with allies whose governments he deplored.

One day as Bartlett sat on a stone bench by a quiet temple in Kyoto, he put himself on trial.

The clerk with a large nose and slicked-down hair proclaimed like a quiz-show emcee, "Let's have a big hand for Judge Bartlett." Behind Bartlett, the audience rose and clapped and cheered as the judge strode into the florescent, vinyl courtroom.

"Thank you, thank you, folks, please be seated," twanged the effeminate clerk.

The judge's jowly face was particularly unsuited to the absurd wig that flopped a bit askew on his triangular head. Judicial wigs with curls should never be worn by people with large noses. And those robes! Look at those robes. A pretty shabby attempt at Joseph's coat of many colors with all those moth holes.

"Will the defendant please," the judge started in an affected, prep school voice, "*GET OFF HIS DUFF!*," and giggled coquettishly at the slick clerk. Bartlett stood, out of fright.

"I believe you wrote your own charge. Let me see now. I had it here . . . Oh yes, here it is. You are accusing yourself of murdering loved ones, supporting deplorable wars, engaging in aggressive, provocative acts with fascist accomplices. My, my, that's a very serious complaint, young man."

Assuming a deep dignified tone, the judge looked over his half-moon glasses. "How do you plead, Patrolman Bartlett?"

"What! I am a lieutenant in the United States Army," objected Bartlett angrily. An old lady in pastel tennis shoes twittered from the jury box.

A tired indulgent expression fell over the judge's face like a venetian blind. "You are one of the policemen of the world, my boy. Now, how do you *PLEAD?*"

Bartlett felt sick. What an absurd court! That ridiculous pompous judge. And look at the jury. They all look alike, just dressed in different rags. That little old lady who keeps muffling her giggles behind a psychedelic handkerchief. They ought to have her replaced. Bartlett wondered why his defense attorney had not seen to that. He looked around at the prudish man, a smile properly fixed on his pale lips, his face etched with the lines of too much whiskey. The court-appointed counselor seemed on the verge of sleep. It was too tiring to ask him.

"I asked you, how do you plead, patrolman? Involved or not involved?"

"WHAT!" Bartlett was thunderstruck. "What kind of raw . . ."

"Ah, ah," the judge cut him short, raising a reproachful hand, "We'll have no more of *that* childishness. It's clear from your behavior that you're involved. Does the jury concur in the verdict?" He cocked his head shyly at the jury.

A bald man at the end of the jury box rose. Oversized pants held up by wide pink suspenders covered his fat frame.

"We . . . dooo . . ." he stammered.

"But he has not even polled the rest of the jury," shouted Bartlett, jumping up and pointing a finger at the jury. The youth felt like rushing over and punching him in his big fat nose.

The judge ignored the outburst. He reached into his drawer and took out a pinch of snuff. He sniffed and sneezed into a towel-size handkerchief which had been racked on the wall behind him, and then modestly threw it down a pneumatic tube by his left foot.

"The evidence having been presented," the judge wheezed, "the verdict having been proclaimed, punishment will be as follows. Will the defendant please rise." The "please" was accentuated as if the judge was drained by the tiresome outbursts of this recalcitrant.

"Having been declared involved in all charges, this court,

after due deliberation, sentences you to go free." The judge raised the hatchet and brought the blunt end down on a square of lead. "This court is abrogated *sine cura*." And he walked out with his nose in the air, taking long awkward strides. The greasy clerk held up a large sign which read APPLAUSE and the audience jumped up cheering and clapping.

III TOKYO

In the boisterous Asakusa section of Tokyo, beyond the striptease houses and peddler stands, there is a small Buddhist temple that is not very famous. It is quite old to be sure—over three hundred years—and has a superbly tranquil garden. But the scene is improved upon many times over in Japan, and outside of the aging women of Asakusa who worship in its stark hall and the scrubbed rosy-cheeked girls who play hop-scotch, Japanese-style, on its stone walkways, the temple has no particular significance.

It was a bright, though unseasonably chilly fall day in 1967 when a tall slender American girl made her way through the crowded streets of Asakusa toward the temple. She towered above the squat, stump, thick-legged Japanese, and as much as their sense of etiquette allowed, they turned an eye to watch the striking girl pass. She was dressed in black—long knee-length boots without heels and a wool coat whose collar she grasped tightly about her neck. She did not seem to notice the attention. She moved through the crowd purposefully, with lengthy strides, her lithe frame a bit stooped as if in self-consciousness for her uncustomary height.

Past the gray wooden gates of the temple, she paused a moment under an oak tree to pull her collar closer about her throat. A pool of yellow and brown leaves surrounded the spot where she stood. And then she moved on, her large brown eyes scanning the garden—not so much, it appeared, in appreciation of its loveliness, as in search of something definite. At last she seemed to find the object of her search, and her pace quickened. She made her way toward a marble bench whose back was etched with graceful Chinese characters. It was set back from the narrow pathway in a small glade of maple trees.

On the bench slumped another American. His hands deep in the pockets of an oversized military coat, his head crouched down to take full advantage of its warmth, he had been there some time now, lost in the memories of a past love. Was it over? Can love lie dormant like a virus, swimming around in the blood stream, waiting for that special stimulus, or does time break it down and make one start all over again? How wonderful that she had suddenly burst forth in Japan, just when he needed her most. When the news had come through a letter from his mother, he had literally run across the BOQ quad, nearly knocking down a major, to the telephone in the opposite building. Had she followed him to Japan? No, she could not have known that he was to be transferred. And *he* had called her, not the reverse. She had said over the phone that she had been in the country six months. So she had arrived several months before he had—about the time when Chuang was boarding the sub. The idea of seeing her again dizzied the young American. He had arrived early so that he might compose himself for the meeting. He was used to being alone there.

"It's not that cold, Lieutenant." The girl's deep voice pierced the silence of the garden almost sacrilegiously.

"Maria?" Bartlett came alive, and he reached out to her. There was an embrace of old friends.

They looked at each other for a moment as if in search of an instantaneous comprehension of what had happened in nearly two years of separation.

"You're a woman now," Bartlett blurted out enthusiastically, and Maria laughed, though with a trace of embarrassment.

"Yes, Jon," she said quietly, looking into the green eyes she remembered so well, "I am a woman now."

"Come, sit down," he said excitedly, grasping her arm and guiding her to the bench, and starting to babble like a fifteen-year old. "Maria, it's so wonderful to see you. I can't tell you how often I've wished you were near, how often I've seen your face in the movies, in the streets, in the mannerisms of a thousand girls."

"Really, Jon. You should be ashamed. Thousands of affairs in two years. My, you are a soldier."

"Well, if you live on the edge of life all the time, like we do. . . ."

She looked at him in playful disbelief. "You . . . on the edge of life . . . You're too smart for that," and then she dissolved in a peal of laughter.

Bartlett joined her.

"But you haven't been to Vietnam, have you?"

"No."

"Thank God for that anyway. Your mother has worried so much about that. They should end this war if only for the mothers of America."

"How is she?"

"She'll be better when you're home. And your grandmother keeps asking when Jonny is coming home from the war."

"She never could distinguish between Vietnam and the Army in general."

"She's not the only one . . . But anyway, some people at home thought you would run off to the jungles to prove yourself or something. You do such crazy things sometimes, Jon." And she kissed him on the cheek.

"And you Maria. Have you been worried too?"

"Now, Jon, it's too soon to be sentimental."

He looked at her, almost in wonderment, a half-pained, half-joyous expression on his broad face. "To think," he muttered, "I left you for the Army . . . my God."

She sensed that it was not a playful remark.

"Perhaps we've both grown up, Jon. I am a woman, and you . . . you are no longer trying so hard to be a man."

Bartlett nodded silently, gazing at this woman, whom he had longed for for two years, who could have had his child, and now . . . she was almost too good, too perfect, too formidable.

"Come," he said finally, trying to break his own spell, "I'll show you my garden." He reached for her hand and gently pulled her up.

"Do you like my temple?"

"It's lovely, Jon. Of course, I have my own favorites."

"Look, the pond is shaped like the character for heart. Did you notice?" He crouched and sketched the character in the sand with his finger. "See?"

"You forget that I'm a student of such things now too. But you win. I hadn't noticed it here. There are some lovely gardens designed like that in Kyoto."

"In your university days, Maria, you would've been impressed that I knew the character for 'heart'."

"I'm not so easy to impress now."

"Just think, you wouldn't be in Japan now if it hadn't been for me—I mean, you would never have become interested in the Orient."

"Perhaps," she replied putting her arm through his, and glancing at him playfully, "but you'll have to keep up with me now."

The two strolled slowly around the pond, past its miniature pagodas and sculptured trees, peeking into the barren polished interior of its hall. They spoke mainly of Maria's life in Japan—her studies under the foremost Oriental art historian at Todai, her volunteer work for the Quakers, her social life with the activists of the university. She was not lavish in these descriptions, but the idea of the active life in politics, art, and the university thrilled Bartlett. It was what he wanted for himself.

After a time Bartlett proposed that they have sake and raw fish at a local sushi shop, and then go on to his favorite quiet jazz coffee house in Shinjuku. Maria agreed happily. His suggestion reminded her of his enjoyment of proletarian locales, surroundings where the common people whom Bartlett neither knew nor understood frolicked without inhibition.

The sake warmed Bartlett and Maria, and they began to display their language ability to the customers. The nimble-fingered sushi-maker explained his trip to the Tokyo fish market that morning as he shaped the rectangular lumps of cold rice and slapped a slab of raw fish on it. His conversation did not slow down his production, and the customers leaned over the counter to listen to the Americans. Before the couple left, a businessman had invited them to a night club, and a student had invited them to his favorite coffee house, but Bartlett demurred graciously; and Maria, who really wanted to accept both invitations, did not object, out of politeness. Bartlett had been so adamant.

Bartlett's exuberance seemed to evaporate as they left the busy shop, and he became silent as they took the train to Shinjuku and passed through the crowded gay streets to his coffee house. They were escorted to a dim corner, and Bartlett ordered several scotches.

Maria wondered if this sudden silence after such elation was the beginning of one of those depressions that she recalled with such horror.

"Jon," she said, reaching her hand to his far cheek and turning his head toward her, "don't wander from me."

He looked into her lovely, sparkling eyes. The dim reddish light illuminated half her face. "It's just that you're everything I ever wanted, Maria, and I'm all clammed up. So much has happened to us both in these two years, and yet we're acting as if we were at the Cleveland Zoo yesterday, bouncing peanuts off the bears and gawking at the orangutan."

Maria smiled and lowered her head onto his shoulder.

"We'll have to get to know one another again," she said.

"Will the Army get in our way?"

"Oh, Jon, the main thing is that you're here. You're here, and alive, and it makes me very happy."

"I've had a tough time of it so far, Maria. It's all my fault, but it has been tough."

Maria seemed not to have heard; her eyes wandered to the dim form of the waitress scurrying about in the smoky red room.

"I'm so ashamed of some of the thoughts I've had about you in this time away," she said. "I've imagined you as a killer when I saw pictures of Americans tagging prisoners, or read stories of assassinations. I'm so ashamed of those thoughts now that I see you. I was so afraid of your becoming brutalized—I suppose more afraid of that than your getting killed. And now when I see you, you look different. Your hair is shorter, your eyes don't have the boyish sparkle they used to, you're thinner, and yet . . . and yet, Jon . . . you are the most exciting person I've ever known."

Bartlett drew her to him, and they kissed, long and deep as if two years could be bridged, dismissed, relived in this one ascendant disconnecting act of love. Their lips finally parted, and Maria slumped breathless to his shoulder.

Neither spoke for a time, and then Bartlett burrowed his face in her hair.

"Do we still have a chance?" he asked.

"We will always have a chance," she answered, raising her lips to his neck. "But first we must discover what we have become."

"I'll try so much harder this time."

"Such bad times were mixed with the good before, Jon," she said pulling away. "And always the worst were when you would not talk to me, would not spill out what was bothering you. It was so poisonous when you kept your problems bottled up under pressure."

"I'll never know why you took it so long, Maria. And then . . . the child."

"Oh, there were some benefits."

Bartlett was pleased.

"But even when we were close, I possessed only a fraction of your thoughts. That's such an incomplete feeling for a woman. I wanted to reach you. I wanted to know you completely. And yet I could never seem to get to you."

"I want you to have those things, much much more than ever before."

"Perhaps it will be possible now. You need me. I want to know why. But I can wait.

"Do you think you can?"

"I've waited this long. Perhaps I have infinite patience."

Bartlett was silent, for he knew it wasn't true.

XII

Bartlett and Maria Hemmings saw one another every night in the week after their joyous reunion. They laughed and skipped through the liveliest streets of Tokyo like children, alternating nights doing what the other wanted to do. They went to plays and museums, mixed with the people in the sushi shops and the socialites in the night clubs, invited themselves to a tea ceremony, and got booted out of a nude photography parlor when Bartlett tried to stop one girl from whipping another (this time Maria could laugh at his puritanism), and stayed up till five one morning to go to the central fish market as the night's fresh catch was brought in.

On the seventh day it was Maria's turn again, and she suggested that they go to the Beeto, a small basement coffee house in Kanda, a student section of Tokyo. She would introduce him to her Tokyo milieu, she told him proudly. He would enjoy her friends, for they had the qualities that he had so appreciated in college. They were extravagantly free and alive, she said, and she was sure this was where his heart was. Bartlett admitted that he wanted to unwind, to throw off all that encumbered him, to race and jump and dance again through a field of flowers in glorious irresponsibility.

The couple picked their way through the crowd in Kanda. Maria pulled him along by the hand, and then pointed to a mauve neon sign—a black musical note and the figures "Beeto" written as if with the stroke of a brush. She led him down the narrow wooden stairway and they emerged into a dimly lit small L-shaped room. The jazz was good, and the coffee rich and thick. All the ingredients for good conversation were there.

As they entered the room, a cry came up from the corner. "Oii, Maria. Over here," came the voice through the smoke and music from a circle of students. Maria had become a thrilling new asset to the Beeto circle, for the Japanese students saw in her a refutation of every idea of womanhood they had been taught from childhood. They were awed by her height, her exotic beauty, her aggressiveness. They were able to shed their self-consciousness with her, to joke and compete with her on an equal level as they had with no other woman in their lives. She would swish into the room and shouts of greeting came from every corner. She knew them all.

After a wave to her admirers, she turned to Bartlett, smiling. "Come on, Jon. I'll introduce you."

"Kenjiro, hi. Hello, fellows. Aren't you going to make room for us? Come on, Taka, be a gentleman."

"Your friend?" one of the students asked, a broad challenging smile on his face.

"No, my lover, silly. Here, move over. Now, this is Lieutenant Jonathan Bartlett, U.S. Army. The shaggy-haired one is Kenjiro, then Takahashi, Fujio, Makato, and Minobe. You can call him Skinny Minny."

Bartlett nodded to each.

"You in the Army now?" Skinny Minny asked.

"Yes, I am," Bartlett answered trying not to be too officious.

"He is an intelligence officer," Maria piped in, "What do you think of that, Fujio?"

"Mmm."

There were nervous glances between the students and then at Maria, but only joy registered on the girl's face.

"Well, don't just stare. Aren't you going to order us a

sake? I thought I taught you better manners than that, Ken."

Warm sake was brought. It was first-class and still had the scent of the cedar barrel. After several cups Bartlett relaxed a little.

Where's Shige?" Maria asked.

"At a meeting in Todai."

"Will he be here tonight?"

"He says so."

"What's the meeting at Todai about?"

Again there were glances at Bartlett and back to Maria.

"It's all right. He's not going to tattle on you. Are you, Lieutenant?"

"No."

"It's about Oji."

"Did the pro-Communists show up?"

"I think so. Oji will be tame. I think they will join."

Lt. Bartlett wondered if they could be talking about Shige Toshikawa, the head of KAKUMARU. He had read about this young revolutionary in the newspapers and in the background documents for his present operation. Several Diet members had felt compelled to condemn officially his disruptive activities. Not much was known about the youth personally, for he seemed to surface only in time of trouble.

"Who's Shige?" he asked Maria innocently.

"Who *is* Shige?" Maria passed the question on to Takahashi.

"Shige is a student at Todai who's occasionally active in politics."

"Is he your leader?" Bartlett asked; Maria smiled in anticipation of Takahashi's answer.

"We have no leaders in KAKUMURU," Takahashi answered, "but Shige is often consulted, more than others as you shall see . . . and very shortly . . . Oii, *koko*."

A striking young student had just entered the room. He was dressed in a suede jacket and tight pants, with a long scarf around his neck. He was tall for a Japanese, nearly as tall as Maria. Maria watched the youth make his way toward their table; he might have been a work of art—his face the doing of a fine sculptor of simple yet powerful works; his dark eyes formed from the smooth skin by one perfectly controlled swipe of the palate knife; the full lips shaped by El Greco fingers.

His arrival caused a stir in the Beeto. He was immediately pelted with questions about the meeting at Todai. He did not answer as his eyes rested on Maria and then moved to Bartlett. Maria got the point.

"Oh, Shige, I'm sorry. This is Lieutenant Jon Bartlett of the U.S. Army. You're under arrest."

"What!" Shige leapt back and stared wide-eyed at Maria. Maria threw her head back in a peal of laughter. Shige did not understand and looked at the others, who were no help.

"No, no, I'm just joking. Come on, sit down. Shige dear, you're so tense nowadays."

"Maria, sometimes your sense of humor goes right over my head," Shige said, relaxing but still piqued.

"I am sorry. Poor baby. But, Shige, you mustn't take yourself so seriously all the time. Radicals in America have nervous breakdowns constantly from such intensity."

Shige chose to ignore the comment and turned to Bartlett. "I am Shige Toshikawa," he said with a slight bow of his head.

"Pleased to meet you, Shige. I'm Jon Bartlett. I'm glad to see that I'm not the only one who's the brunt of Maria's teasing."

"Is it so that you are in the American Army?"

"Yes, it is. I'm in for exactly ten more months."

"I see."

"He is an intelligence officer," Takahashi said to Shige in Japanese."

"*Soo desu ka.*" Shige nodded thanks to his compatriot.

"Oh, Shige, you mustn't be so suspicious. Jon was something of a radical when he was in college, weren't you, Jon? He is responsible for making me aware of a lot of things . . . including politics."

"I see," Shige said. "Do you find it difficult being in the Army now, Lieutenant Bartlett?"

"Yes, often it's very difficult."

"I mean, do you have questions of conscience about it? For example, I understand a majority of the American people want to bomb North Vietnam into oblivion, and many favor using the atomic bomb. Such solutions to Asian problems seem to come easily to Americans."

"Not many. Some. I don't favor these solutions, and yes, occasionally, I'm not so proud to be in the Army."

"And last week, I read in the papers that the Americans are on the verge of an invasion of North Vietnam. An Admiral Sharupu hinted it in Hawaii."

"Admiral Sharp?"

"Yes. How do you feel about that?"

"I think it would be a mistake."

"It would be a mistake all right, but must a soldier not believe in what he does to be a good soldier?"

"No, I don't think so," answered Bartlett not really wanting to get into the subject. "It's like being skilled on the lathe in a big factory. You run the lathe efficiently as you've been taught without reference to the overall operation."

"Then what's the point of taking the risks? Surely not the money, which is why one would work in a factory."

"That doesn't come into it. You follow orders to be a good soldier, and that's all."

"I think it'd be easier to believe."

"Soldiers are not supposed to be concerned with belief."

"That's not what America told Germany and Japan after the Second World War."

"That was different."

"I don't understand you, Lieutenant."

How could this Oriental understand, Bartlett wondered silently, when he himself did not? "One does not talk about a good soldier anymore. The slogging dogface GI is out. It's the professional soldier now. He pursues his duties with diligence because he's professional and has pride. He's the efficient specialist, a skilled laborer, thoroughly trained, coldly efficient. The Pentagon has adjusted its methods to the different mood of its soldiers very cleverly. Uncle Sam used to point out from the poster saying, 'I WANT YOU.' Now he says, 'I WANT YOU—IF YOU'RE GOOD ENOUGH,' as if the business was something to aspire to."

"So they devised a virtue of professionalism in the absence of the virtue of patriotism?"

"And it has worked. Haven't you seen the reports of the old war correspondents from Vietnam? They're all impressed with the change in the American GI. He's better equipped, better trained, better supplied with cold beer in his strategic hamlets, and he complains less. Perhaps belief makes a lousy soldier, especially if it has to replace starched fatigues and cold beer."

"Of course, there's the VC," said Shige.

"Some say that's fanaticism."

Bartlett was embarrassed at his comment, and the conversation lapsed.

After a time Minobe broke the silence.

"What do you think would happen if all of a sudden soldiers did start to think and believe? What would the politicians do for their armies if it weren't for innocent kids who believed their stories about romantic glory or virility and poor kids who were tempted by the inducements of military pension plans, PXs, and free housing?"

The vision of Jacques LaCompte from Houma, Louisiana, crossed Bartlett's mind. In basic training, the seventeen-year old had explained that he volunteered to be a helicopter gunner because his recruiter had compared the killer job to riding shotgun on the pony express. Bartlett thought of the officers from small Southern colleges for whom the Army provided a measure of dignity and of the slovenly sergeants who fed on this welfare system of the uniform.

"What do you know about it?" he said rudely.

Shige smiled. He sensed that the American was agitated.

"I'll tell you a story, Lieutenant. I have an uncle who was in the Japanese Army in World War II. He was attached to a headquarters garrison in Hankow in 1944, when he learned that a push south to Indochina was going to be made. There were many stories among Japanese soldiers in those days about Hong Kong tarts in Kuelin. The town in Kwangsi Province was a major American stronghold then and would surely be a big objective of the southern thrust. I suppose my uncle was curious about front-line action and he probably half expected that there would be a prolonged orgy of victory in Kuelin as there'd been in Nanking in 1937. Anyway, he deserted his rear-line post in Hankow and made his way to the front. He ended up with the advance in Kuelin all right, but he was wounded there, captured by the retreating Chinese forces, tortured by them, and ended up in a Russian concentration camp in Sakhalin for four years."

"And so?"

"Perhaps if he'd believed in victory in Kuelin, or if he'd been convinced that the Emperor really needed him there, and if later he hadn't been convinced of the foolishness of his act, he would not be such a bitter man today."

"What is the point, Shige?"

"Oh, Jon, don't act so stupid," Maria mumbled almost under her breath.

"The point is the absurdity of risking life on a childish impulse or for an anti-ideal, or for a vainglorious national delusion. The point is that each poster in America flashing virile, romantic military figures should be answered with the charge of propaganda; that each plea to fight Communism should be answered with 'What better alternative do you offer?'; and when a cabinet member falls back in moral defeat on the argument of national interest to justify a war, the individual should reply, 'In that case, I'll serve my own personal interest.' "

"And what would you say is in my personal interest now?" Bartlett asked them all plaintively, imploringly, almost pathetically, but not really expecting an answer.

"Did you ever consider doing what Maria's brother did?"

"What about Bruce, Maria?"

"Oh, Shige, is all this necessary? We were having such fun before you came."

"What happened to Bruce?"

"He applied for CO status a year ago," Maria began sullenly. "At first he felt that he was a conscientious objector only against the war in Vietnam. Once he took that position toward Vietnam, he decided it was where he should have been all along on all wars. Well, I don't know what he will do when the draft notice comes. They're not granting CO status any more, you know."

"Tell the lieutenant what he wrote you, Maria," Makata spoke up for the first time.

"You tell him."

"He wrote Maria, 'Just think, if I'd been draftable two

years ago when I was eighteen, I'd have been out shooting up the Cong with fellow high-school study . . .' "

"Stud friends, Makata. How many time have I explained that to you." Maria frowned, her eyes fixed on her sake cup.

"He continued, 'I'd never have confronted the issue!' "

"Don't you see, Lieutenant," Shige said, "What's happening in Vietnam is too grotesque, too insane. There's no more point to fine discussions. Everyone knows where they stand. Only action gives importance to belief now."

"That's easy for you to say," Bartlett said without looking at Shige.

Maria looked at Bartlett, for the first time, a pained expression on her face. "Oh, Jon, has two years so changed your ideals?" The others raised their eyes to Bartlett.

"Look, Maria, I'm a lieutenant in the U.S. Army. That means I can get hung for any action that does not jibe with the Army's method of achieving peace. I'm for peace too. So are a lot of people in the military. Everybody's for peace—until they have a chance to participate in a war. What if your heart and your mind pull you in opposite directions? What if your heart says the situation demands revolt and your mind can't disentangle the situation in any meaningful, realistic way. Then what?"

"I'll tell you what you do in the event of that conflict," Shige replied to Bartlett's growing hysterics, "you choose the higher law, the higher impulse, the higher loyalty." He paused. "And if you're worried that my position is emotional, I don't deny it. The emotional postion is the only valid one anymore. The burden doesn't rest on me to articulate reasons why the killing must stop. It rests on you to explain why it must go on."

"Do you think it's fun for me to deal in death and destructiveness and weapons all the time?" Bartlett lashed back. "Do you think I enjoy bowing and scraping and following the orders of men I have no respect for?" He was almost shouting. "I understand your hostility toward the war. My God, I share it, but what's your message? What's your alternative? Peace? What does that mean? What principle would you have every American soldier follow? Desertion? Treason? Betrayal? And what kind of society and world order would that leave us with?"

The students sat stunned in silence and disbelief at this display. Bartlett looked frantically at each, enraged at their lack of understanding, and at himself for wasting his thought on them.

Maria leveled an anguished stare at him, deep disappointment registering on her flushed face.

"You haven't changed in one way, Jon," she said slowly and sadly, tearless. "You're still intent on analyzing every question into the ground. In the end you scratch your head and watch everyone else pass you by."

She paused. "That's what happened to us two years ago. You analyzed us right out of existence."

Maria and Bartlett left the Beeto several minutes later. After a silent cab ride through the dark streets and a perfunctory goodnight, Maria walked alone to her door. Bartlett directed the cab to the 243rd Detachment, woke up the staff duty NCO, and signed himself in.

"Going to work at this hour, sir?" the bleary-eyed sergeant asked, trying to be nice and at the same time divert attention from his dereliction of duty.

"What's it to you?" Bartlett quipped. "The CO will hear about how tired you are, Sergeant."

He climbed the stairs, walked to his desk, and then opened the safe. Taking out a long sheet of paper, he walked to his typewriter and set to work.

INTELLIGENCE INFORMATION REPORT

Classification: CONFIDENTIAL
Source: 1
Reliability: A
Priority: Bravo
To: Commanding Officer, Det Seacrest
From: Jonathan Bartlett, First Lieutenant, AIS
Subject: Shige Toshikawa, leader of KAKUMURU . . .

It was not really ethical, Bartlett thought as he began banging the keys, but it's an imperfect world any way you look at it.

XIII

Those entrusted with the awesome responsibility of the leadership of our nation deserve not only our support, but our rejection of those in our midst who would arrogantly kibitz in a game where they haven't even seen the cards with which the game is played.

—GOVERNOR RONALD REAGAN

But what I fear most is that for lack of a political choice in 1968 there will be a large exodus from the political arena into some form of political nihilism—despair, drugs, withdrawal, sporadic violence, refusal to play the game, including attempts to break up and interfere with the game.

—WALTER LIPPMANN

In the few weeks that followed the disastrous evening at the Beeto, Bartlett lapsed into a sullen sustained depression. He could not bring himself to call Maria for a few days, and when he finally did he pleaded with her to forgive him for his silly display. Several days had been enough to calm Maria's anger and embarrassment at the interchange between Bartlett and Shige, and yet it could not be forgotten. Maria wondered what it all meant, what possibly could have happened to Bartlett in the Army that would launch him into such hysterics.

When Bartlett hung up the phone after persuading Maria to meet him the following night, his thoughts drifted to Shige. Was it enough to apologize to Maria? Hadn't he acted like a fool in front of Shige as well, and wasn't this an interesting young ally whose friendship would be valuable and stimulating? And then in an exhausting wave of remorse and guilt, Bartlett remembered his report. Pelsey had been exuberant about it. Shannon would be readying it for publication within the intelligence community by now, and adding it to his list of accomplishments.

Wasn't this how the Chuang affair started, Bartlett wondered to himself. Hadn't he allowed the Army to use his grounding in philosophy and politics and Oriental culture for its own purposes? Of course, he had consented. And look what the result had been! Could he let them do the same with Shige? And when his relationship to Shige was based on his relationship to Maria? It was too nightmarish. Bartlett shuddered at the subtle savagery of it all. Hastily he scrawled off a note of apologetic explanation to Shige in Japanese, and then lay down on his bed and went fast asleep.

The meeting with Maria the following evening was to set a pattern for the next months. The two went to a movie and then had a sake before an early parting. The confrontation with Shige was not mentioned, each dreading the other would broach it, each preparing what he or she would say if it did come up. Their discussions were polite and dull. They scrupulously avoided the sensitive sources of hurt or affection that could have brought them together.

Neither Bartlett nor Maria quite realized the impact of this poisonous internalizing of their differences. Bartlett sensed Maria's withdrawal, but misinterpreted it as a temporary pique, a woman's mood, that she would get over as she always had done in their rocky periods in Ohio. Maria waited for Bartlett to come forward with the apology and the explanation she deserved, and her pride told her not to force the issue.

When Bartlett did not open up to her, she began to notice qualities in him that she found deeply disturbing. He often talked of how hard his job was, what strains it put upon him and how he sometimes feared he would crack under the pressure. When she asked why it was so hard, he always demurred with innocuous evasions about stupid superiors or the dirty jobs they gave young lieutenants. It seemed to Maria that his philosophical bent that had drawn her to him first had soured into sadness, even self-pity.

Maria in a last desperate attempt to destroy his tense secretiveness began to ply him with questions about his past. If he would only open up about that, perhaps they could come to an understanding, she thought. Yet when the explanation finally came, it was hardly a comfort to her. They had been in a coffee house in Asakusa, close to her flat, when Bartlett said softly, this time without prompting and without looking at her, "I killed a man in Taiwan, Maria."

His sentence struck Maria just as his hand had struck her two years before, and she looked at him wide-eyed, catching her breath, her hand going to her cheek as before, with the same shocked expression of disbelief and pain.

It is difficult to say why Bartlett chose to reveal the Chuang affair to her that way without elaboration. He did it on impulse, not calculating his comments as he had become so used to doing. Perhaps he felt it was the most honest way to describe his moods. Perhaps he even felt that Maria would sympathize with his anguish over Chuang, and help him work it out. But he was as naive about mature women as he was about his exploitation by the military. For, beyond her physical beauty, Maria had become a woman with complex emotions, a commitment in life, a delicate balance that would not be trifled with now as it had been before. And nothing could have hardened her quicker than to view Bartlett as a killer, a trigger-man, an executioner, standing arrogantly over the body of a lifeless, ragged Oriental. His comment restored the grotesque fixations about him that she had suffered in her nightmares in their two years apart, and which she had attempted to smother in Japan.

Several days later Lt. Bartlett was given the word that Lt. Col. Pelsey wanted to see him. There had been an odd shuffling about in the office that day. The lieutenant, though he had noticed it, did not have the energy or curiosity to rouse himself from the thick CISCO document on Chicom radar types. He knew from experience that he would find out soon enough what the stir was about.

Lt. Bartlett made his way dazedly down the synthetic hall to the CO's office, his mind processing the radar data by remote control and racing ahead to a further radar study he would propose to Pelsey as an operational aid to Chinese penetrations.

He knocked once and then opened the door to find the entire detachment crammed into Pelsey's small office.

"Oh, excuse me, sir." Bartlett said, and started to back out.

"No, no, come in, Captain." There was a big laugh in the room. Bartlett looked around the room at the smiling faces and then back at Pelsey's impish face.

"Well," he said, breaking into a broad grin and striding into the office, "thank you, sir."

Lt. Col. Pelsey gave a short speech, saying that Capt. Bartlett was the only soldier he had ever commanded who aspired to be a Renaissance man. Since that was true, he, Pelsey, had done some research, and wished to point out how far Bartlett had to go. Then Pelsey went into a short diversion about Lorenzo Battista Alberti, one of his heroes, the first great architect of the Italian Renaissance who not only built beautiful buildings near Florence, but wrote novels and philosophy, composed music, taught himself physics, mathematics, and canon law, but most importantly (to Pelsey) could tame wild horses and jump clear over a man's head from a standing position. (Bartlett looked up the man later and found Pelsey had the first name wrong. It was Leon Battista Alberti.) And then Pelsey mentioned Bartlett's last report, which had gotten top evaluations from USARPAC, DA, and CISCO. Pelsey praised the report as an example for the other men.

The speech over, the bars were affixed to Bartlett's shoulders. He smiled at his friends through the ceremony, embarrassed and flustered by all the attention, thanked everyone, but insisted that he still was not going to make it his career. Everyone laughed, and the coffee and cake were brought in by the Oriental office boy.

After the ceremony Bartlett was given the rest of the day off, and he decided to wander down to the Ginza to an English bookstore to look for one of Suzuki's books on Zen and to check Pelsey's research. Half-consciously, he neglected to change into civilian clothes, and he occasionally glanced to the shiny new bars on his shoulders. He began to browse in the store, and after a time, he sensed the gaze of another browser on him. He looked up. It was Maria.

"You look brutal enough," she said, then turned and walked out of the store. Shocked at first, he could only gape at her as she left, and looked around to see if other customers had heard. When he recovered, his impulse was to run after her and say, "No, no, you don't understand. It's not like that. It's just a job. One day follows the next." But it was no use.

What had happened to the pride and respect that was supposed to accompany the sacrifices of soldiering? The captain was confused, but he dared not ever allow himself to be seen by the girl again in uniform. He hurried back to the base to change, and then he called Maria. Wouldn't she please meet him in his garden in Asakusa? He pressed her, and she relented reluctantly, almost tearfully.

By the time Bartlett arrived in Asakusa, the gray cold day was on the wane. As he entered the wooden gates and scanned the garden for Maria, he sensed that winter had conferred an icy inhospitality on his haven, and he shuddered a bit. The trees which had blazed in such wondrous fall lustrousness when he had been here on their first reunion, now were bundled up against the cold with wrappings of straw. A raven cawed in the bare branches overhead.

Maria was already there, sitting on the edge of the same marble bench. She watched him enter the garden from the gates and make his way along the pathway that traced the fringe of the heart pond.

"Hello, Maria," he said, as she rose to meet him, and then adding almost businesslike, "can't we go somewhere else—somewhere warmer perhaps? The garden seems so cold and unfriendly this afternoon."

"I don't think there's much point, Jon. I can't stay long anyway. There's a meeting tonight."

"Maria, please, tell me what I can do. I can't lose you like this—not without a fight, without knowing why."

"I don't see the point in analyzing it, Jon."

"It can't just be the uniform. Baby, I belong to you. I'll do anything for you." The words came hard to Bartlett, for he was used to being on the receiving end of such pleas.

"It's just that I can't bear the thought of you as a killer anymore. It's just too much for me, Jon."

"But it's not exactly that way, Maria . . ."

"I've always loved your sensitivity, your love of beauty and nature and ideas. But all these seem to have been cancelled out somehow."

"No, Maria, they haven't been cancelled out. Believe me. You'll see. You'll see when I'm out of the Army. Only eight more months. Then there won't be any more pressures, no more secretiveness. You'll see that things haven't changed. Please give me a chance."

"I can't wait eight months."

"But Maria, can't you try to appreciate my position? I'm not free. I could ruin my whole life just to please you now. And then what future could we have?"

"In eight months another seven thousand Americans will die in Vietnam and kill ten times as many Vietnamese. Shige says as long as fifteen hundred soldiers die a week, the American government loses its right to be interesting. Its betrayal is too great. It must be destroyed."

"Oh Maria, that's drivel! Surely you see that."

Maria looked at him disapprovingly, silently, not deigning to reply.

"Then what do you propose to do?" Bartlett asked, looking away from her to the pathway.

"Shige says that shocking the American people is the only method left."

"And how do you and Shige plan to do that?" The outlines of a smile traced Bartlett's full lips.

"Well, you can tell your intelligence connections that I'm going to work for KAKUMARU in Yokosuka and Sasebo, urging American soldiers and sailors to desert. Shige thinks I can be effective."

Bartlett endured a miserable silence, and then he mumbled, "I'm sure you'll have no trouble bending the average GI."

"It's not just the average GI we're after. We'll be talking to officers just as intelligent as you, Jon."

Maria slipped off her black glove and rummaged in her purse for a cigarette. Bartlett found a match and lit it with his cold hands.

"Don't you see," she said, "I have made my choice, and you evidently have made yours. I thought, or I hoped at first, that the Army and the war would make no difference. But I was wrong. It's too important to me."

She looked at Bartlett's sullen face. "I'm sorry, Lieutenant. . . . Captain." She rose and glanced back at him. "Goodbye," she said, and flipped her cigarette into the pond.

TROOP INFORMATION — Block 3

MESSAGE FROM THE COMMANDER IN CHIEF: 21 MARCH 1968

Persevere in Vietnam we must and we will. There, too, today we stand at a turning point. The enemy of freedom has chosen to make this year the decisive one. He is striking out in a desperate and vicious effort to try to shape the final outcome of his purposes.

So far we think he has failed in his major objectives. He has failed—at a terrible cost to himself and a tragic cost to his civilian victims.

I saw General Westmoreland's report this morning and he shows since the Tet period, 43,000 of the enemy have been killed and 7,000 have been captured. He has lost 50,000 men since that holiday period began—because thousands of our courageous sons and millions of brave South Vietnamese have answered aggressions onslaught, and they have answered it with one strong and one united voice: "No retreat! Free men will never bow to force and abandon their future to tyranny."

That must be our answer too, here at home. Our answer here at home, in every home, must be: "No retreat from the responsibilities of the hour and the day."

We are living in a dangerous world, and we must understand it. We must be prepared to stand up when we need to.

There must be no failing of our fighting sons!

There must be no betrayal of those who fight beside us!

There must be no breaking of America's given word or America's commitments! When we give our word it must mean just what it says. America's word is America's bond. Isn't that the way **you** feel about it?

There must be no weaking of the will that would encourage the enemy or would prolong the bloody conflict!

Peace will come of that response, of our unshakable and untiring resolve, and only of that. The peace of Asia and the peace of America will turn on it.

I do not believe that we will ever buckle. I believe that every American will answer now for his future and the future of his children.

I believe he will say, "I did not retreat when the going got rough. I did not fall back when the enemy advanced and things got tough, when the terrrorists attacked, when the cities were stormed, the villages assaulted, and the people massacred."

I think every American would want to say: "Where was I? I stood up to be counted. I stood fast beside my brothers and my sons who went away to fight for me. I stood firm with my Government to fight to preserve the way of life that we hold so precious and so dear.

XIV

Here we have bookish dreams, a heart unhinged by theories. Here we see resolution in the first stage, but resolution of a special kind: he resolved to do it like jumping over a precipice or from a bell tower and his legs shook as he went to the crime. He forgot to shut the door after him, and murdered two people for a theory . . . but consider this: he is a murderer, but looks upon himself as an honest man, despises others, poses as injured innocence.

—FËDOR DOSTOEVSKI, Crime and Punishment

Perhaps his parents erred when they protected Jonathan Bartlett in his early years from those hardships that steel men for tragedy or ambiguity in life, and nurtured at the same time a philosophical cast of mind, untempered by experience, that interpreted acts in moral terms. Anyway, the young man was fat for the kill when it came.

The violent scheme of things into which the young officer had been drawn was, to be sure, of a lesser order than some members of his generation had endured. Bartlett had not pulled the trigger of the gun that severed Chuang's head from its trunk. And there was only one death to feel guilty about. Yet Bartlett was denied the argument that "it was either him or me," and he saw no meaningful difference between the act of killing and the act of causing death.

It is said that with time men get over the obliviousness to the death and destruction of war along with the springlike tautness that combat produced in them. Time had passed for Bartlett, however, and—perhaps because his emotions were more subtle and less dulled than the average infantryman's; perhaps because Maria, whom he deeply loved, and Shige, whose ideas and activism he profoundly respected, exerted such a strong emotional pull on him now—his preoccupation with the past and with his continuing military involvement became greater rather than less.

Yet this preoccupation was not enough to chart a clear course of action. For the soldiering instinct was deeply ingrained in Bartlett. He took his business seriously. He respected orders and the responsibility of command. He was romantic about those who risked their lives for an ideal—any ideal—and he took pride in his ability to bring imagination and flair into a business usually so flat and unproductive.

And so Bartlett reeled through a chaos of bewilderment and disillusion, developing a dual life between the office and the Beeto coffee house, chasing after Shige's ideals and Maria's elusive affections by night, adopting a correct, efficient military posture by day, but questioning his motivations night and day. Could he trust his instincts? Shouldn't he wait until the whole brutish experience faded into dim memory? After all, he had only eight months more, and then his whole life lay ahead of him. And what about the instincts of Shige and Maria? Didn't they too want his services just as the Army wanted them? What then was the difference?

Had it not been for one devastating incident in February, Bartlett might have continued his tortured indecision indefinitely. The news was full of gory details of the Tet offensive in Vietnam. The soldiers at the 243rd Detachment in Japan buzzed about nothing else on their long coffee breaks. The offensive shocked Capt. Bartlett by its vicious brutality, and his heart went out to those under fire.

During the height of the enemy attacks, Capt. Bartlett sat in his cubicle staring out the window, the morning edition of the Japan *Times* covering his desk. He wondered what Shige would be saying about the news that night at the Beeto.

"If you have a headache, today is not the day to get it cured at Oji," Bartlett was snapped out of his daydreams as Capt. Paul Dalton relaxed his giant frame into the gray chair by Bartlett's desk. Dalton was from Brooklyn, a pleasant, well-organized officer with an easy nature, the sort a girl could use as a brother in stormy times. The two officers had been trained together and worked as a team. Bartlett had taught the Brooklynite not to drop his *tt's* when he pronounced *cattle* or *bottle.* Dalton in turn looked out for the forgetful and flighty Bartlett in the trivia of military life. Small oversights could cause such trouble for a soldier. There were no secrets between the two men in such close quarters, and Bartlett sometimes thought that had its bad aspects.

"Oh, why is that?" Bartlett asked indifferently, to be polite.

"Because they're bringing in the wounded from Hue. They're stacked in the halls with tags on 'em like some goddamn veterinary hospital."

"Were you up there?"

"Yeah. Sure picked a fine day to get my shots updated."

"You know, Paul," Bartlett said, leaning back in his chair, "Hue is the only place in Vietnam that ever seemed in the least bit romantic to me. It has such great names: the Citadel, the Perfume River, the Bridge of Golden Waters, the Palace of Perfect Peace, and the vision of sensuous Vietnamese kings and queens. It's the only place that seemed to have a little dignity in all that squalor."

"Well, I wouldn't get too romantic about it now, old boy. The whole fucking place will be leveled before this one is over."

"So much for Vietnamese history. The South Vietnam Interior Department will have a hard time setting up historical monuments after this war."

"The South Vietnam Interior Department is the secret police."

Bartlett thought it was time for a change in the tone of the conversation. "Do you know anyone in Hue?"

"I'm not sure. All I know about Weinstein, Schoop, and Jones is a drawer number for their mail. They're somewhere in the boonies, could be Hue. Oh, and there is Rolland. I think you met him on Sword Island. He was a funny kid. I remember when I got orders to language school in Monterey, I asked him about hiking in the Sierras and about the Big Sur. He took basic at Ord, you know. He said he didn't know much about hiking, but he could suggest a most outstanding Mexican whorehouse in Seaside. Funny kid. And he used to go out with the *ugliest* women you've ever seen. Big fat slobby things with foul tongues. . . . 'Course nowhere in Nam is good right now. Every place is getting hit."

"I didn't know you knew Ray. It'd be a hell of a thing if he got hurt. He wrote me a few letters trying to justify volunteering for Nam—stupid things about the benefits of PX privileges, choice of stateside assignments afterwards, chance really to get involved. The main reason he went, though, was he couldn't stand Shannon. I wonder if he regrets it now."

"Say, you know what else they're talking about at Oji. There's some chance that the Japanese radical groups are going to demonstrate there because it's a U.S. Army Hospital treating the Vietnam wounded or some such crap. Have you heard anything about that in your operation?"

"There have been some noises about it."

"You know they're saying something else pretty clever. They're arguing that Vietnam casualties are bringing in exotic jungle diseases that will spread through the surrounding neighborhoods. No slouches, huh?"

"Maybe they're right."

"You wouldn't say that if Weinstein or Rolland were being treated in there for Vietnam wounds and radicals were busting up the place."

Bartlett decided Dalton had a point.

"But I'll tell you something, Jon." Dalton's eyes wandered out the window. "I'm confused in my own mind about these radicals, just as I am about American GIs who desert. I can understand their confusion over the war."

"Well, congratulations."

"No, really, you've got to respect them."

"Ah, come on, Paul. What if everybody acted like the radicals, as you call them, or all soldiers took some actions against their Army. We'd have chaos, maybe more wars and more violence than we already have." Bartlett was probing, still only half-interested in the conversation.

"Yeah, but what if nobody took action. Look at it that way. Johnson and his military machine would be in North Vietnam with an invasion tomorrow morning and hitting Chinese nuclear targets by the afternoon. These kids here and at home who protest, the GIs who drop out, maybe they're the ones making the history. All we do is sit in our comfortable chairs, complain about how horrible the war is, and do our job efficiently."

"Ah, come on, Paul, it would be totally absurd for one of us to do anything."

"It would be totally absurd, sure, but some people are doing that very absurd thing. They're the ones, not us, who are saying to the higher-ups that maybe you can't quite trust this younger generation anymore to do your dirty work."

"Easy now, young man, don't be ideological. You never know who may be listening."

Bartlett's comment did not quite succeed in covering his agitation. What right did Dalton have to run him into an advocate for the system? He knew that Dalton, who was gaining a reputation as one of the smoothest operators in Japan, was exercising these arguments just to show that he was up on things. Maybe he was even sounding out Bartlett for the security branch! You couldn't trust anyone anymore. And yet Dalton was expressing Bartlett's own dilemma. How humiliating for this professional to be saying these things, when Bartlett knew Dalton did not feel the dilemma deeply. Bartlett resented him for it.

There was a hesitant knock on the door and Corp. Harvey Schwarz appeared. Schwarz was the source of constant amusement to Bartlett and Dalton, for he was always in trouble. A sensitive kid from Flatbush, Schwarz wore a peace medal under his fatigues. He had been the courier in the unit until the MPs caught him drunk in bed with a fifty-five-year-old Korean woman in Shinjuku one night. He was put in the mailroom after that. His latest trouble had come when he punched a master sergeant for calling Martin Luther King "a natty nigger." Dalton and Bartlett had gone to bat for Schwarz, and thereby earned the corporal's eternal thanks. Pelsey had found the incident mildly amusing and let Schwarz off with a fatherly lecture on striking a superior. To show his thanks to the young captains, Schwarz kept them informed of backdoor politics as it passed through the mailroom in the form of confidential notes.

"Scuse me, sir, but I taught you'd be interested. Der was a back channel message come in from Nam dis moning. Don't tell nobody I toed ya now. It'd be my ass again."

"Let's see it, Harv."

"I wrote it out on dis here piece of paper."

Bartlett absorbed the crooked letters of Harvey's scrawl slowly.

Hue detachment of 230 MI captured by VC today. Extent of compromise not known. Five officers taken prisoner: Majs Crockett & Tanimura, Capts Freehan & O'Bannon, and Lt. Madras. Lt. Ray Rolland killed by groin and face wounds while looking out window when first shots fired. Information will be kept classified eyes only to protect intelligence connections of captured officers from enemy.

"Thank you, Harvey." Bartlett said calmly and handed the message to Dalton.

"Be sure you tear dat up now, else ah'll be in nother military hurt."

"Sure, Harv." Bartlett nodded, and Schwarz left.

Dalton looked up from the message, stunned, a sick look on his face.

"You remember what they told us in advanced training, Jon," he mumbled. "Nobody in our job gets killed in Vietnam. It would require too much paperwork."

"Yeah," Bartlett replied, getting up and starting towards his commander's office, "that's what Rolland said."

"Chief," he said as Pelsey looked up, "I got a pretty bad headache and a few chills. Probably that skiing in Hokkaido last weekend. Like to take the rest of the day off."

"Sure, Jon, need a doc?"

"No, thanks, I'll pick something up at the PX."

Bartlett walked impassively out of the office and across the post to the BOQ and there vomited into the toilet bowl.

The days following revealed little further information about the circumstances of Lt. Rolland's death, except that the bullet that struck him in the eyes had been a ricochet. The fact of his death remained classified, not only to protect the intelligence connections of the captured U.S. officers, but also to prevent any leakage to the press about the destruction of the Army's intelligence capabilities in the North. Ironically, Rolland's Hue detachment had precisely predicted the attack on Hue, but for some reason had not taken measures to protect itself from the attack it knew was coming.

And so Lt. Ray Rolland would never be honored in Rock Springs, Wyoming, as a war hero struck down in glorious combat. A Defense Department representative sneaked into town with the news for the parents and asked them to keep it to themselves. People on Main Street in Rock Springs would only whisper and gossip about what happened to Mrs. Rolland's boy.

The Tokyo Detachment of the 243rd exhibited a tempered reaction to Lt. Rolland's death. Was one allowed to grieve? What measure of sorrow was permissible? No one was sure since no one was supposed to know he had been killed. Ears were alert for an indication from the command. It soon came. The security officer put out the word to his informants that any conversation about Rolland was to be reported to him. He would "get" anyone who broadcasted the leak. But the younger officers like Bartlett and Dalton who had known Rolland the best talked about it heatedly among themselves for days. In general, however, after some emotion at first, the soldiers put the incident out of their minds. After a time mention of it was considered poor taste.

Capt. Bartlett stayed away from duty for three days on the pretext of a stomach virus. No one questioned or particularly cared about his motives. It was during this period, sometimes sitting wide awake in the darkness of his quarters, sometimes lingering over a sake in Shinjuku, that he decided to act. With all the thorough attention to detail that the military had taught him, he began to plot the course of his conspiracy.

In the days that followed his return to duty, no one noticed anything strange about Capt. Bartlett's behavior. He questioned various colleagues about their activities in Tokyo and on missions to other places in the Orient. But Bartlett had always been curious, and his friends were glad to oblige. He carried on his work with his customary diligence and even worked some evenings. Occasionally in the morning his face appeared pale and drawn, a state which any one would have attributed to a late evening in Shinjuku. Soldiers in Tokyo were supposed to do that sort of thing.

For a month after the news of Rolland's death, Bartlett spent most of his time in his quarters or in a demure Japanese inn in Asakusa, bent over a sheaf of papers written in Chinese or Japanese. To the plump, fawning proprietress of the inn, he was a diligent student of Oriental language. Occasionally, he put in an appearance at the Beeto, but even Shige with whom Bartlett's relations were now formal at best, found the soldier's behavior strange. Bartlett asked Shige about a few Thai, Burmese, or Vietnamese students at Tokyo University. Where Bartlett had gotten the names, Shige did not know. But he became suspicious and decided to search out the students. They all said that Bartlett had come to see them, and they had helped him write some letters in their native language. But they would not tell Shige the content of the letters. This bothered the young revolutionary all the more.

During this period, in the wooden cubbyhole of a post office several blocks from the Asakusa train station, the mama san who was the post mistress began to see a thin Westerner on a regular basis. Every third day or so, just before closing time, the fragile glass door would slide open, the Westerner would duck so as not to hit his head, and then bow slightly, saying politely, "*Konnichi wa.*"

He would then stand patiently in line. And when he was first, he would inquire about the mama san's health with a smile. She would bow and thank him, and then he would hand her a letter, bound for an address in Japan or another Asian country, and always written in the native language. After a month or so of this activity, the mama san began to joke with her customer. "To what honorable place do we travel today?" The eyes behind her circular, wire-framed glasses were friendly.

"Today to the land of flowers and honey," he would reply and then bid her farewell.

But Bartlett did not come by his treachery easily. His tension and excitement grew as time passed. Occasionally at night he suffered from stomach cramps and chills. It became harder to maintain his front at work.

And then, two months after Rolland's death he exploded.

The occasion was one of Lt. Col. Pelsey's briefings with his officers. The 243rd had suffered several serious setbacks in their operations in the previous three weeks. Pelsey had received one of those "Dear John" letters from Shannon, telling him to "get with the program." Shannon himself was being pressured by CISCO and higher headquarters for an explanation. Pelsey was passing everybody's frustration on to the next echelon down.

The scolding followed traditional lines. Operations were discussed one by one. Pelsey tossed in his barbs, jibing at individual officers for unprofessional techniques, generalizing the mistakes of one officer into lessons for all. There was no defense in the face of the colonel's thrusts. But he defeated his own purpose. His contempt for the whole organization, his acknowledgment of the fruitlessness of his prodding came through in his snide comments and cynical laughs. Bartlett, once a fresh breeze in the 243rd, had joined the defeated in Pelsey's eyes. His performance had gone down since his promotion. Pelsey had begun to regard him as just another moldy fixture in the musty room.

Capt. Bartlett slouched in the corner of the briefing room. He no longer made an attempt to be bright and enthusiastic at these meetings. Other promotion-conscious officers assiduously took notes as if this would impress Pelsey. Bartlett felt he could remember if something important came up.

Pelsey moved on to the next item scribbled on his legal pad. This time he got Bartlett's attention.

"A wave of emotion swept through here two months ago with the news of Lieutenant Ray Rolland's death in Hue. I know that some of you knew him well. I did not say anything at the time, partly because there's not much that can be said, partly because several other members of his team were captured by the enemy alive. Now I've heard the talk about why Rolland left this unit, what a waste he thought it was, and what he felt about Col. Shannon.

"Well, gentlemen, this is an old story. People get into wars for all kinds of crazy reasons and some get hurt. As long as there are nations with conflicting ambitions, as long as there are aggressive groups and rebellious groups in this world, and as long as governments keep secrets from one another, there will always be rubouts. Vietnam only reflects an imperfect world. It's too bad it had to be Rolland. He was a nice boy. But he was involved in a big job.

"Last night I was watching the news on TV. There was a picture of a Negro marine behind a wall in Hue. The reporter asked him what he thought of the Vietnam situation. He said,

'The whole thing stinks,' and then he stuck his head up above the wall again and resumed his firing at the enemy.

"All I can say, gentlemen, is that I hope you think of Rolland and that marine the next time you gripe about your work around here. At least nobody's shooting at you. You work more or less regular hours and go home to nice little houses. The closest you get to combat in Tokyo is the fireworks at the Obon Festival.

"I want you to take Rolland's death as a stimulus to get more operations going and to improve the ones you have. This is the smallest kind of tribute that we owe to Ray Rolland. If we can do this, perhaps his death won't have been in vain."

Pelsey paused and looked aound the assemblage to gauge the effect. His eyes fell on Bartlett, who was sitting straight up in his chair. There was a wild crazed look on the captain's face, and Pelsey looked away a little embarrassed.

The words formed slowly on Bartlett's lips, first in a whisper. "I . . . can't believe it . . ." Then more audibly, ". . . I don't believe you could use Rolland's death that way. . . ."

He whirled around and walked out of the briefing.

Capt. Bartlett hurriedly pushed a path through the rush-hour crowd, jostling with the confidence of a giant those who did not make way. He might have been considered simply a rude foreigner had he not been in uniform. It was no way for an American military officer to act in a foreign country. The blank faces of the downtown Tokyo shoppers turned to watch this curious undignified soldier and assumed that some urgent matter of state hung in the balance.

The captain was oblivious to the scene he was causing. He had to get to Maria to tell her that he had finally taken his step, that there was no turning back now. How would she react? Would this finally, at long last, dissolve the barriers between them? Would she accept him now? He pushed on through the subway station to the Asakusa train amid the grunts and reproachful grimaces of the faceless Japanese.

Outside the Asakusa station a line of minicabs hustled to pick up customers. The captain brushed past the orderly queue and, with a perfunctory smile and a quick apology to the startled gentleman at the head of the line, crunched his thin frame into the small back seat of the cab. He reeled off the address to the driver. "*Asakusa 2 Chome, 11–16 e itte kudasai.*" What a stupid address system this town has, Bartlett thought. Now someone else could do his rushing for him.

The cobblestone streets of Asakusa were alive with the mad competition of Japanese urban traffic, as the flimsy cab threaded its way through the mess, darting, retreating, feigning, honking. Bartlett warmed to the spirit of the match. He wondered if there was not some way to help the driver spot the quick openers. The hawkers in the small shops and concession stands along the main street, flogging octopus cakes or raw squid or some steaming concoction, were moving into their evening tone of voice. Altogether the vibrant sounds of the modern city filled the dreamer with a momentary excitement and pleasure.

At Maria Hemmings' flat Bartlett barked the order for the cab to wait and received an obedient nod and a clipped "*Hai*" from the driver. He had been here only once—when Maria had made green tea, and they sat on her straw matted floor, talking about temples in Kyoto with strains of ancient Bunraku music in the background. The rooms were part of a house owned by a professor of physics at Todai, who had insisted that the corner room of the apartment, which looked out on the Japanese garden, remain in the simple Japanese style. Maria was delighted to comply. After long deliberation she had chosen two large scrolls that dominated the dais of the tatami living room. One was of a plum branch in blossom; the other of an oak tree, its branches painted with strong strokes, leaves fanning out at its base. Below the dais Maria had placed cushions carefully to afford the best view of the garden. In the small back room which served as her bedroom and work room Maria had hung up a large poster of Jeanne Moreau. On the fringe of the mirror above her cosmetics table she had small pictures of Che Guevara, Jean Paul Belmondo, Cary Grant, and Bartlett. The two rooms, she told Bartlett, allowed her to travel from Western to Eastern civilization according to her mood.

The light wooden door to the back entrance slid open easily, and Bartlett briskly made his way across the flat stone walkway. The pebble garden had not been raked that day. He knocked. No answer. Again. Nothing.

The captain pondered the situation for a moment. Returning to the cab he directed the driver to an address in Kanda, a section of the city noted for its book stalls, where many students including Shige lived.

Again the minicab sped off with an urgent roar of the motor, and the soldier lounged back in a vain attempt to relax. Lining the cluttered streets, the stores, packed with foodstuffs, magazines, electronic gadgets—whatever would satisfy the appetites of the populace—became a blur of color, a smudge on a sooty, ricecloth canvas. Look out! A middle-aged woman stepped from the median between the two lanes of frantic traffic, clutching a purple cloth wrapped around something square. The cab swerved slightly to the opposite side of its lane without slackening its pace. Bartlett looked into her eyes as she passed going fifty miles per hour. An amused, not frightened expression. Just testing. She trusted him!

Click—120 yen.

What was it like to end a life prematurely at fifty-five? The cab driver raced on, immovable, unfeeling, inscrutable behind the white sanitary mask that covered his nose and mouth: protection against the impure, foreign odors floating around his cab. What was his rush? At least Shannon and Pelsey would have a hard time trailing this cab. Imagine an Army sedan racing through Tokyo after this guy! Bartlett looked around. Only cabs and empty trucks under the cold gray sky.

Click—200 yen.

A tiny, three-wheel truck nudged into the lane. Good luck, mac. The will of the masked madman is iron. To lose a life at fifty-five. The cab approached the flank of a cyclist; one hand held the handlebar, while the other supported a tray piled high with porcelain tea cups and a steel pot. Better than at twenty-seven. Bartlett turned to get a look at the young face. Athletic, hard. What did he have to look forward to?

Click—270 yen.

The taxi stopped in front of a flat yellow apartment house. The low horizontal lines of its four stories had allowed the architect to achieve a certain density of habitation by thinner stories when earthquakes would not permit him height. Bartlett expected the ceilings to be four feet high. He counted out the exact change and then taking the steps four at a time raced up to the third floor in anticipation of conferring the glorious news on Shige.

At the door he knocked quickly twice and without waiting for an answer burst into the darkened smoky room. The scene that greeted Capt. Bartlett was as much a surprise to him as his appearance in uniform was to the gathering of radicals. In the center of the matted room the students kneeled over a low round table with a large map of Tokyo draped over it. Several students wore the yellow helmets of construction workers. Their design was similar to the U.S. Army combat helmet liners. A wan shaggy-haired student crouched in a corner with a four-foot wooden stave cocked like a baseball bat, ready to attack the intruder. Bartlett recognized him as skinny Minobe. Behind the student some forty newly cut staves were stacked neatly in the corner. From there the arsenal expanded: boxes of stones from a railroad bed and chunks of concrete, three crates of empty beer bottles, strips of cloth, a large red tin can, and a helter-skelter pile of helmet-liners and towels. On the bare concrete walls of the apartment bold slogans had been painted in red and black with passionate strokes.

SMASH THE RIOT POLICE

DOWN WITH AMERICAN IMPERIALISM

Bartlett stood speechless, paralyzed. Finally, he brought his eyes back to the table. Facing him across the map, in the midst of the assemblage was Shige, and draped over his spare shoulders, slightly out of the beam of the shaded lamp which hung from the ceiling by a thin strand of wire, was Maria.

There was a painful moment of silence. Finally, Bartlett stammered, "Shige . . . I'm sorry to . . . Well, I just wanted to talk to you about something important. . . . I didn't know you were . . ."

Bartlett's ineptness seemed to snap Shige out of his astonishment. He collected himself quickly. Motioning to the shaggy student in the corner to put down the stave, he turned calmly back to Bartlett.

"Are you here in an official capacity, Lieutenant?"

"Oh, no, I just didn't have time to . . . change." Bartlett felt ashamed in his costume.

"Well, then, since you are dressed for the occasion, perhaps you can act as our military adviser. We haven't had such an impressive figure in our midst in quite some time, not since the commander of the local riot police was here three months ago."

"I doubt that I could . . ."

"Nonsense. You are too modest. We're preparing for a demonstration tomorrow morning against the American military hospital at Oji. These are the squad leaders of my platoon, and of course, Maria, who is, shall we say, my lieutenant. You have been to Oji, I believe. Perhaps you can confirm our information about the entrances to the building. Should we get past the police barricade tomorrow, we will need to know how to get inside."

"What is the point of . . . getting inside?" Bartlett was still somewhat in a state of shock.

"What an odd question. To smash as much as we can and then get out. For an educated man and a military officer you're very naive, you know. We intend to make it so unpleasant for the American military that they will wonder if the cost of supporting the Vietnam war from Japan is really worth the effort. You might call it *our* 'war of attrition' or 'raising the price of American aggression' or even a demonstration in support of the 'freedom-loving peoples of South Vietnam.' Nice concepts you Americans have given to the world. The only problem is that they can be turned against you. Oh, you needn't worry, Lieutenant, it is not likely that we will breach the police phalanx. They usually set a troop superiority ratio of three to one."

"You needn't call me Lieutenant, Shige . . ."

"Ah, yes, I think Maria told me you had been promoted. Congratulations."

"It's not that. I may not be in the Army very much longer. That was what . . ."

"How interesting. Fancy that, Maria. In that case you

will have fewer compunctions about helping us plan tomorrow's festivities. Regardless of your present status, you are highly trained by the best military professionals in the world. And so we have a problem which should delight your military mind: how to assault a police cordon inflicting as much damage as possible, with a minimum of casualties. Naturally the more effective our assault, the more effect it will have in the press and in American military circles, and the more chance there will be of the government overacting."

"Shige, I've . . . I've never heard you talk like this before. You sound like my superiors or like President Johnson."

"You needn't mention President Johnson in this room. If he came to Japan, he would be beaten to death with staves like those in the corner over there."

"Please, Shige, don't push me like that. What happened to the principles we talked about over coffee? The violence you are talking about is what I am fleeing. Don't you see, I'm through with the cold calculation of violence. Now you drag yourself down to their plane. What moral influence can you have with such tactics? You offer them the luxury of dismissing you as another unruly mob. They will say you must be suppressed for the sake of social order."

"I think it would be best if you remove yourself altogether from modern politics—er, Major, is it? If the military has brought you to such an abhorrence of violence, then you are not able to deal with the world as it is and with the techniques that are required to change it for the better. What is a political philosophy without realistic political action? It is meaningless. What we talked about in the coffeehouses was rubbish without tomorrow's demonstration. If we sound like your superiors, you sound like the ruling class. 'Suppress the unruly, violent mob,' he says. If that is your order of values, rather than 'Down with the War in Vietnam' you too must be smashed."

"I can't change the impact that the military has had, Shige. You may be right that I should remove myself from modern politics, but your tense is wrong. I should've removed myself three years ago. Now I'm trapped. But I won't compound my stupidity by lending my military skills to your battle with the police."

Bartlett looked to Maria. She regarded him, emotionless, in judgment. And then he turned toward the door.

"So you snivel and employ your military arts for the U.S. Army," Shige sneered after him.

Bartlett turned back to the group.

"You missed my point, Shige. That is over with also. That's what I came to tell you and Maria."

It is also true that in the presence of revolving injustice the only honourable attitude is revolt—but if one compares the noble ideals in the name of which revolutions were started with the sorry end to which they came, one realizes that a polluted society pollutes even its revolutionary offspring.

—ARTHUR KOESTLER, Arrow in the Blue

In Oji, a northern section of the city, the Tokyo Riot Police, the Kidootai, were preparing for the next day. The Oji U.S. Army Field Hospital occupied a sooty cement building that had been an ordinance arsenal for the Imperial Japanese Army before the big war. The installation was not difficult to fortify, for just outside its main gate there was enough space for a crowd to gather. Wooden shacks and unpainted tenement houses pressed in on the remaining sections of the hospital's perimeter.

Outside the two gates, Kidootai troopers in blue fatigues were stringing rows of concertina as their first line of defense. The ends of the barbed-wire coils were fastened to wooden poles implanted in the cracked, grimy street and then spiraled in dual rows across the broad entrance. More wire was strung over the concertina rolls and held erect by unsecured wooden poles, so that when the job was done, the attacker was invited into an amorphous mire of concertina—a jungle of unpredictable barbs. The riot police knew the technique of defense well. They had done this many times before. And, of course, the defense of military installations in Vietnam had done much to advance the state of the art.

As the specialists prepared the physical defense of the hospital, the stark chief of the Kidootai handled other logistical matters. Police intelligence, on the strength of information from student informants, estimated that a mob of fifteen hundred would storm Oji Hospital the following morning. Consequently, the chief issued mobilization orders for four thousand riot policemen. The equipment was made ready: helmets with plastic face-masks, three-foot night sticks, padded jackets and gloves, reinforced leather wrist and arm protection, large nets on bamboo poles, body-length aluminum shields with eye slits which had recently replaced the heavier, less mobile leather variety, tear-gas cannisters, gas masks. Things were proceeding smoothly at Central Headquarters in downtown Tokyo. By dusk the situation was under control and coordination with the U.S. Army Japan Command was completed.

Throughout the night a tight security watch was clamped on the installation. Vietnam wounded were diverted to other U.S. Army hospitals in the Far East. At 0700 the Kidootai deployed, eight deep at the entrance with a three-man cordon around the entire fence, and several units of two hundred men each held for quick deployment at any weak spot in the perimeter.

At 0855 the eerie chants of the students could be heard in the distance, mingled with short blasts from a plastic whistle. The Kidootai chief put out the alert along the line from his command post on the fourth floor. At 0910 the first platoon of students emerged from a small winding walkway, four abreast and twelve deep, arms intertwined, and snake dancing past the main entrance to the hospital. The students all wore helmets which bore in Chinese characters either the name of their radical faction or the dictum, "anti-war." Tucked under the light straps of these helmets, old towels of wadded cloth covered their faces below the eyes, giving them a masked, almost pagan, anonymity useful in such situations. Despite the constant carping from squad leaders on the side of the formation, the students carried their staves at odd angles—a sign of poor discipline and insufficient training.

The platoon surged forward in a slow trot, chanting to the whistle blasts of its leader: "*SMASH AMERICAN IMPERIALISM*," "*PREPARE FOR STRUGGLE*," "*CRUSH KIDOOTAI*," "*ON TO FINAL VICTORY*." The chant was echoed by other platoons that were now converging on the target from other narrow streets. Huge red banners began to appear in the growing sea of helmeted students, screaming venomous slogans against the American war and Japanese involvement in it.

LBJ MURDERER
SATO—LACKEY OF AMERICAN IMPERIALIST DOGS
DARE TO SNATCH OKINAWA

Flag bearers waved their banners with slow reverence, defiantly, before the coils of concertina. The cruel, angry sea of sticks, banners, and multicolored helmets undulated with fearsome noise—howling, screaming, hooting, desperate with excited anticipation.

All the while, as the army of students swarmed around the main gate, one platoon leader, distinguished only by the tiger colors of his helmet, appeared to be the focus of command decisions. Now when it looked as if the attack was imminent, this student was suddenly hoisted onto a comrade's shoulders; a portable loudspeaker was produced from somewhere, and he began a speech.

"*REVOLUTIONARY STUDENTS*. Today we continue in the great struggle against bourgeois capitalism and American imperialism. . . . This struggle only begins with the expulsion of the American militarists from Japanese soil. . . . It will end only when Japanese culture is purged of its bourgeois and militarist tendencies. . . . The struggle is international. American, Czechoslovakian, French, German, and Russian students fight alongside us. . . . And it is an existential and metaphysical struggle. With each confrontation we grow stronger, purer, better prepared for the final victory."

The harangue had no pianissimo or fortissimo. Each sentence gushed over the crowd with the same vehemence. Each last syllable lingered and died out as if it were a full note at the end of a musical phrase. The speaker had his audience. His mention of the metaphysical struggle brought in unison the thunderous approbation, "*YOSSHH*."

"We are the new authority . . . We are the conscience of this nation that has no faith . . . Who else will stand up to the American imperialists . . . Who else attacks the decadence of our country . . . Who else attacks the neocolonialism of America and Japan . . . Who else?"

"*YOSSHH* . . ."

"The poor people of Oji support our struggle against the Oji Hospital. . . . From this hospital Americans spread their jungle diseases through Oji just as from Japan and Okinawa they spread their disease of neocolonialism and cultural degradation through Asia. *THEY MUST BE STOPPED*. . . ."

"*YOSSHH* . . ."

"There is only one way . . . *SMASH AMERICAN*

BASES IN OJI AND NIPPON AND OKINAWA . . . SMASH YANKEE DESIGNS AGAINST ORIENTAL PEOPLES . . . ON TO DIRECT DEMOCRACY . . ."

"*YOSSHH . . .*"

The students now began to take up the chant, raising their fists or staves at the end of each slogan: "*SMASH KIDOOTAI*," "*SMASH AMERICAN IMPERIALISM*," "*SMASH THE SECURITY TREATY*." The tiger-helmeted rebel led them with his loudspeaker, and the noise grew deafening.

Tense, the police watched as their adversaries began to swell and surge around the entrance. Only a few minutes of horrible tension elapsed before the violence broke out, and they were the worst of all. After the missiles started to fly over the barbed-wire barricade into the police phalanx, everyone seemed to slip naturally and calmly into their respective roles. The nets were raised in front of the defenders; the water was turned on the attackers. Still the tinkle of glass or a metallic thud could be heard at unpredictable intervals as rocks found their marks on the hospital windows or the water-spraying truck.

The special operations unit of KAKUMARU now deployed to the wire, first throwing ladders onto the barricade and then, farther down the fence, beginning to cut the concertina. Brave student commandoes like Vietcong sappers moved onto the uncertain footing of the ladders. The first few fell screaming into the fearsome entanglement and others moved to take their places. Several did make it across the barricade and waded into the police lines swinging their long staves. Quickly they were subdued and whisked off to an unknown confinement.

The commando action appeared to have succeeded as a diversionary tactic as the special operations units were making headway in clearing a hole in the wire. Another diversionary action also became important at this point. From a small side street and hidden from view, a special squad from a stone-throwing unit began to hurl molotov cocktails into the rear and the flanks of the police lines. This necessitated the re-direction of the water-spraying operation away from the main attack to the task of extinguishing the splashes of fire amidst the police lines.

Finally a hole in the wire was cleared and the attack elements swept through the breach yelling frantically, ecstatically, at the top of their lungs. There was an awful clashing of staves and wooden clubs mixed with grunts and screams and the thuds of wood on plastic or aluminum, as police and students engaged in hand-to-hand combat.

Rocks and pieces of concrete rained down on the police lines almost as if the students had called in artillery on their own positions. Young girls rushed in ammunition on stretchers from a rear-area supply depot where a sidewalk was being broken up. But now the rocks began to have a great effect, for the attack elements had torn down the large net that had intercepted the barrage before. To the amazement of all, especially the students, the police began to retreat.

It was at this point—this glorious moment of exaltation when the students found themselves with the initiative—that the tear gas cannisters began to explode. The elements had been kind to the police that morning. There was no wind and the cramped nature of the surrounding buildings trapped the tear gas as if in a vacuum bell. For a moment the assault stalled as the students adjusted towels around their faces and pulled ski goggles or skin-diving masks over their vulnerable eyes. The poisonous white smoke rose with slow inevitability until it was impossible to see more than a few feet.

Suddenly through the fog of tear gas a legion of policemen appeared from nowhere. In helmets and the gas masks with their swinging trunks of oxygen, they became a hideous apparition of some grotesque race of two-legged beasts. The front line pushed forward with their body-length medieval shields. Those students who saw the counteroffensive before it was on them—many students were bent-over, coughing or clutching at their burning eyes—cracked their staves futilely against the sturdy shields. The police waded into the broken student ranks, clubbing wildly at any unfortunate who had not been chased back by the gas. The immobilized were left to be gathered up by the auxiliary rank of police that followed behind.

The situation for the amateurs rapidly deteriorated into anarchy of every man for himself. Some spirited youths who had seen the counteroffensive from the rear now charged the formation individually hoping to get in a lick and then get away unharmed. This technique was quickly repulsed as several policemen would peel off and meet the lone attacker, clubbing him to the ground. After several students were mercilessly beaten and hauled away to the rear, no more such Kamikaze attackers presented themselves.

The fourth floor of the hospital facing the main gate commanded the best view of the action from start to finish. It was here, from the office of the hospital commandant, that the chief of the Kidootai, surrounded by walkie-talkies and American military officers, directed his forces in battle. As a result, the commotion on the fourth floor was tremendous, and the nurses, irritated by the disruption, had to fight their way through the crowd to their patients.

At the end of the fourth-floor corridor and therefore somewhat removed from the battle traffic was the orthopedic ward. Now badly strained with Tet casualties, the ward had declared itself full to capacity. Further orthopedic cases were ordered diverted to Tripler Army Hospital in Honolulu.

It was, of course, impossible for the nurses of the ward to pretend that nothing was going on outside the hospital. The familiar sounds of combat filled the ward. And so, with the constant prodding of the wounded soldiers, the head nurse, Maj. Guinness, finally consented to let the more healthy patients watch at the windows. It was not long before the ward began to swing like the bleachers at a football game.

"Hey, you nips, rip 'em up. Hey, Clancey, look at the weirdo over there." A cast-covered arm scraped against its neighbor as it pointed in the direction of a long-haired sapper who was just about to cross the barricade. "Bonzai, fucker. Oooo. Stupid bastard."

Through the mist of tear gas the police counteroffensive brought those soldiers who could to their feet.

"Go-o-o, get 'em, Hirohito. Hey, those nip cops are pretty good. If the Gook police in Phu Bai were that good, we'd be straight."

Peels of high-pitched laughter resounded through the ward as students scattered and there were more joking comparisons between this battle and the ones the soldiers had experienced in Vietnam. The noise became too much, however, and Maj. Guinness was forced to order the casualties back to their hospital beds.

In the bedlam no one took much notice of a bespectacled officer in a doctor's robe who watched unobtrusively from a corner window. He stood silent through most of the action, behind a very vocal, chubby-faced paratrooper wearing a cast from waist to neck. As the police cleared the street, the young man walked out of the ward, tossing his doctor's robe over a chair by the ward. "Thanks, Major," he said to the horsey woman behind the desk, and proceeded to the back entrance of the hospital. At the back gate he was stopped by a Kidootai sergeant.

"I'm sorry, but you can't leave, sir. It's too dangerous out there."

The young man flashed an identification card. "Intelligence. No time to lose, Sergeant. My commanding officer is waiting for a message three blocks from here."

"Oh, yes sir." The sergeant snapped to attention. "My mistake."

Bartlett looked up and down the line of barbed wire. The street was littered with staves, rocks, broken glass, a few helmets, and bits of torn sheets that had been banners. The faint noise of clashes in the surrounding alleys and windy streets were still audible as the police mopped up the remaining pockets of resistance. But on the immediate street in front of the hospital, the auxiliary police stood idly by in groups of ten or eleven.

In a sweep of the eye, Bartlett cased the situation and then slipped into a side street. The drab wooden houses seemed deserted. The only testimony to life in the apartment blocks was the day's wash that had been hung out to dry on the tiny balconies. Bartlett felt as if a thousand eyes were upon him from behind the laundry or the dark sliding doors of the shacks. He hurried down several blocks and turned into an alley leading in the direction of the noise. The sides of the alley were piled with trash—empty boxes or crates of empty beer bottles. As the soldier moved down the alley, he instinctively identified places of concealment—behind a stack of chicken cages here or a trash barrel there—that he could slip into in case of danger.

Just before the alley issued into another main street, Bartlett heard the clap of tennis shoes against the pavement.

The noise of running grew louder, and the youth slipped behind a pile of wooden fish boxes.

"Here—down here," he heard a voice shout, and past him flew five students, staves still in hand. Thirty meters down the alley they stopped and disappeared from Bartlett's sight behind a pile of trash. One of the students wore a tiger-colored helmet. The American could barely make out their panting whispers. Suddenly two of the five dashed across the alley and again disappeared behind an indented doorway.

The sound of running could again be heard on the street. Bartlett crouched lower behind his flimsy cover. Between two boards of a fish crate, he saw two policemen.

"There goes one. I'll get him." A wispy policeman raced past Bartlett. The other policeman disappeared up the street.

A moment later there was a terrible scraping of leather against cement as the policeman hit the pavement and rolled into the pile of chicken cages. A terrifying scream filled the alley as the students set upon the unfortunate man with their clubs. Thud after thud landed as the fanatical students appeared to have lost all perspective in their orgiasic pounding. One stave broke over the victim's head, and the student reached for a box.

Fright froze Bartlett to his crouching position at first, but as the beating went on for a seeming eternity, he began to come to his senses.

"Stop . . . Stop . . ." he stammered in English, emerging from his hiding place and moving toward the students. "Stop it."

The students recoiled from the bleeding heap on the cement; the one nearest Bartlett in the tiger helmet, sprung into a striking position. It was Shige.

He moved threateningly toward Bartlett. "Get out of

here, you pig," he shouted and took a half-hearted swing at Bartlett.

Bartlett tried to say something, but he choked on the words. He gawked at Shige and then at the bloody heap behind. Shige followed his eyes.

"Maybe he's dead, but don't feel sorry for him, Lieutenant. I'd look for your Maria, if I were you. I lost her three blocks back."

"Maria?" Bartlett gasped in disbelief.

That was the end of it. Four policemen appeared at the far end of the alley. "*THERE THEY ARE!*" and up the alley they came.

The students sped off with Bartlett close behind. At a cross street the students turned right. Bartlett followed. And then as they passed another alley, Shige yelled back, "She's somewhere down there, foreigner."

Bartlett's legs obediently carried him into the side alley. He darted, panting, into a deserted slipway and froze against a dank wall. He waited for the running steps of the policemen. He heard them now, coming closer and closer, louder and louder. He pressed his back hard against the wall.

The policemen raced by. They had not seen him. Bartlett waited for their footsteps to become faint, and then he moved down the trashy alley, slowly, cautiously, prepared for the worst. He passed one alley and then another. No sign of her. And then he came to a narrow corridor. It was a cul de sac. At the end of it, against a corrugated fence a body lay prostrate.

Bartlett raced to it. It was Maria. A helmet was still strapped to her head. A stave lay beside her. Blood formed a small pool below her matted hair.

Reaching down gently with nervous hands, Bartlett unfastened her helmet and lifted her head off the pavement.

Blood oozed from the bridge of her long thin nose and cheek, and the swelling had already closed her eyes.

"Maria," Bartlett whispered. "Maria."

The girl moved a little with a groan.

"Maria, you're going to be all right. I'll go for help as soon as I can."

She muttered something. Bartlett could not make it out. He took out his handkerchief with his left hand and wiped the mess from her mottled olive skin. It occurred to him that the cut would leave a scar along the lovely line of her high cheekbone.

She was dizzy and in a state of shock. How could he get help? He started to rise, but the girl's head slowly reached to his as it rested on her torn cheek.

"Jon . . . they came so fast . . . can't see anything . . . keep spinning," she gurgled through the mess, groping for the arms and the body that supported her.

"It's all right now, Maria. You're going to be all right. Don't try to talk."

"They came so fast . . . I didn't see them. . . . Are you hurt?" She tried to move closer, tried to reach to his face and then louder, a little panicky, "Shige, are you hurt?"

"Relax, Maria. Shige's not hurt. I saw him just five minutes ago."

"Who . . ."

"It's Jon . . ."

There was a silence. It was too much for her—too much to decipher why he was there and how he had found her. It was too much.

"Jon . . . oh, Jon," she reached for him and her hand fell limply against his chest.

"We'll make it, Maria. We'll make it."

Bartlett managed to wriggle off his fatigue jacket, still

keeping her head off the pavement. Gently, carefully, lovingly, he slid the wadded jacket under her head. She relaxed onto it.

"*ASOKO!*" He heard the rasping Japanese at the end of the corridor and swirled around to see two Kidootai troopers bearing down on him with raised nightsticks.

Quickly he reached for Maria's stave and crouched, ready to swing.

"Come on, you slant-eyed bastards," he ground out between his clenched teeth.

The following day, bruised and very sore, Capt. Jonathan Bartlett was transferred from the custody of the Japanese police to the custody of the United States Army. He was held incommunicado for one week.

During this period, through intensive coordination, the Japanese police and U.S. Army counterintelligence brought numbers of loose strands together. The commanding general, United States Army Japan, decided that Capt. Bartlett would be transferred to Hawaii for court martial on four counts of treason and conspiracy. The day he was actually transferred, nearly a month after he had been subdued in that cluttered alley in Oji, Shige Toshikawa, along with three other students, was indicted in a Japanese court for the murder of a Kidootai policeman.

A general outline of the Bartlett treachery follows. In the few weeks after the message about Lt. Ray Rolland's death in Hue arrived in the 243rd, Capt. Bartlett made a surreptitious study of the 243rd's operations in the Orient. He later testified at his trial that he was looking for a very precise thing: any member of his own generation who like Chuang—from naivete, from a desperate situation, or from a sense of adventure—was becoming involved in the U.S. military's or CISCO's scheme of international intrigue. Applying all the skills of deception that the Army had taught him, he wrote letters to these people, in one way or another warning them of the consequences of their involvement. In this way he sabotaged thirty potential intelligence operations from Burma to Japan.

His apprehension by counterintelligence agents revealed the hand of eternal justice. For the same vanity that led Capt. Bartlett to think he could rise above the established rules of nations into some superior justice of his own definition caught him up in his own deceitfulness. He recruited Vietnamese or Thai accomplices from Tokyo University—friends of Shige Toshikawa—to write letters to Vietnamese or Thai youths who were becoming entangled in the power game. But the letters to Japanese or Chinese youths Bartlett had insisted on writing himself. They were masterpieces of fine Oriental script. They had only one flaw. The characters that incorporated the symbol for "mouth," the simple square, the ever so simple square, were always slightly awkward, fatally un-Oriental. Army experts noticed the awkwardness in the week of the demonstration at Oji, when one of the letters was retrieved from a scared Japanese student with a journalist brother in Hanoi.

Captain Bartlett's capture by the Kidootai made everything fit into place.

松本氏へ

前略

おそらく申し上げておくべきだと思うのですが、中部太平洋物産のトムヘムステッドは実はアメリカ軍の諜報員です。あなたもスパイ活動に巻き込まれるおそれがあります。ですから彼とのコネクションをただちに全面的に断った方が良いと思います。さもないと活動に利用され、さらにきがいを加えられるに違いありません。

草々

Dear Mr. Matsumoto,

I feel that it is my duty to inform you that the person known to you as Mr. Tom Hemsted of Mid-Pacific Investments is actually an agent of American military intelligence. You are being drawn into a dangerous espionage operation. My advice is that you sever all connections with him immediately lest you be subject to blackmail and personal injury.

A Friend

HONOLULU

April 1968

Judge:

We teach our children killing. When their
Generosity—bred in tender valleys
Unplundered by the latest robber barons—
Rises against lessons of death, it speaks
Through mouths of revolvers which we taught.
Then, till to maintain the gentlemanly cycle
Of smiling disaster, we execute
Their spiritual will armed against war.

—STEPHEN SPENDER, Trial of a Judge

TROOP INFORMATION — Block 4

PERSONAL EFFECTS INVENTORY
NAVMC 10154-PD (Rev. 9-65)

NAME: Larkin, Daniel F. GRADE: PFC SER. NO.: 2209864 STATUS: KIA

Articles: 1. Ronson lighter, bearing inscription: "Yea, though I walk through the valley of the shadow of death, I will fear no evil: for I am the meanest son of a bitch in the valley."

Q: Governor, could you please outline for us your views on the War in Vietnam?
A: Sure. My position on Vietnam is very simple. And I feel this way—I haven't spoken on it, because I haven't felt there was any major contribution that I had to make at the time. I think that our concepts as a nation, and that our actions are not completely relevant today to the realities or the magnitude and the complexity of the problems that we face in this conflict.
Q: Governor, what does that mean?
A: Just what I said.

WESTERN UNION TELEGRAM

This concerns your the Army will return your loved one to a port in the U.S. by first available military airlift. At port remains will be placed in a metal casket and delivered (accompanied by military escort) by most expeditious means to any funeral director designated by the next of kin or to any national cemetery in which there is available grave space. You will be advised by the U.S. port authorities concerning the movement and arrival time at destination.

Forms on which to claim authorized interment allowance will accompany remains. This allowance may not exceed $75 if consignment is made directly to superintendent of a national cemetery. When consignment is made to a funeral director prior to interment in a national cemetery, the maximum allowance is $250; if burial takes place in a civilian cemetery, the maximum allowance is $500.

Request next of kin advise by collect telegram addressed to Disposition Branch, Memorial Division, Department of the Army, WUX MB, Wash. D.C.

CHAIRMAN, Joint Chiefs: "The War in Vietnam is the foggiest war in my own personal experience."

The huge fiery ball of sun was disappearing behind the western horizon as the insignificant U.S. Air Force C-141 first appeared in the golden Hawaiian sky. The soft low rays of the waning sun had deprived the sea of its azure purity, but still the gossamer frills of the surf danced at the edges of the welcome coast line. The plane began its descent, still far enough away from the approaching island to thread a path through the galleons of cumulo-nimbus that stood in false protection. The folds of the luxuriant mountains darkened in the evening light, and over a distant point a local squall refreshed the cooling vegetation. Over the delicate greenness of the Barber's Point cane fields, over the isolated huts and storage houses in their midst—suddenly the engines of war were everywhere—Pearl Harbor and then Hickam Field.

The plane shook furiously as the engines were reversed, and Capt. Bartlett was thrust against the back of his chair. He felt disoriented being seated backwards like this. The wings drooped down now from the top of the fuselage as the plane slowed and awkwardly turned off the runway toward the command tower. From his window, Bartlett looked out to the hardware: the C-124s, the flying boxcars that could carry three tanks and looked so unfit for the skies, the observation planes with their bumps in queer places for radar, and the Phantom jets, camouflaged in dull greens and browns, all so perfectly in order, all so neatly kept, like the fine cutting tools on a surgeon's side table.

War planes had such personality. They should be able to talk, Bartlett thought. He doubted if he would get on with them very well. The Phantom jets would be conceited like peacocks—always showing off, drawing attention to their good looks, letting everybody know they were the fastest, most efficient, cruelest weapon in the world. He wouldn't have much to say to the fat cargo planes either. They were so slow and dumb; they had no comprehension of what they were doing. "Give me a job an' it's done!" But these large jobs—the C-141s and the B-52s—they were the most obnoxious of all. They always had a mean scowl on their face. When they raced down the runway you knew they were mad. They were out to get somebody, and when they'd knocked him flat with their big punch they'd sweep away with a haughty, smug, filthy laugh.

Bartlett wondered to himself what point these musings had now. He did not need to fight the temptation of the militarist in him anymore. It was all over for him now. When had he begun to think this way? In a flash he remembered and smiled. Maj. Potts, that had been his name. "The capabilities of the B-40 cannon have been well demonstrated in Vietnam . . . Its MRT is . . . meters . . . It is used throughout the RVN in battalion and larger operations . . ." The lecture had droned on. Then the portly major had turned and given a nod. The gun went off with a shattering bang, then the whistle and the billowing cloud of orange and black flame. Bartlett remembered glancing down the line of awed faces—to his toughened skin-headed OCS companions and then back to the self-satisfied look of Maj. Potts. That had been the day he determined always to view the use of these machines as a vulgar extravagance, as a weakness rather than strength.

The C-141 stopped in front of a large tin hangar and Bartlett began to gather his things together. Reaching under his seat he groped for his garrison cap. His hand hit a paper cup. It was a coffee cup that he had placed there and forgotten sometime after Guam. The dregs poured onto his military cap.

"Damn," he cursed at himself. "Typical."

Once on the ground in the warm breeze, flanked by two counterintelligence agents in plain clothes, the captain started toward the hangar.

"Good afternoon, sir." A smart airborne corporal stood before Bartlett in a salute. Where had he come from? A Vietnam combat badge and a purple-heart ribbon were carefully displayed above his left pocket.

"Good afternoon, Corporal," Bartlett said, doing his best to remember how he was supposed to act.

Ahead of them, several MPs and a captain waited. "I'll bet they're for us," Bartlett thought, "and I'll bet the captain's eyes jump to the spot on my cap." They did. It was all so predictable.

Capt. Bartlett's arrest in Japan was quite a jolt to the 243rd. The unit had had to face compromises before, but you plan for a source to double-cross you. An officer—as knowledgeable as anybody in the unit of its operations, one who had been entrusted with vital planning assignments, and who had taken charge of a top-priority operation—how do you plan for his double-cross?

Col. Shannon displayed a new side to his character when the news hit his desk. Maj. Holliwell, the aide who helped the colonel with his English, had never seen fear in the old man's eyes before. When Shannon finished reading the message, he looked up at the toothy major, his face white and drawn.

"You can forget about a future in the Army, Holliwell," he quivered. "The punk from Shaker Heights has finished the 243rd and everybody in it."

As clearly as Shannon grasped in that moment the disaster the compromise meant for his career and his unit, his instinct to protect himself, so central to his military constitution, took hold of him. He had been adept in the past at covering up failure with displays of meaningless statistics or with complicated argumentation. Maybe he could get away with it again. Frantically he worked and reworked his first communication of the compromise to higher headquarters, downplaying the damage and placing it in the category of problems with which the 243rd dealt day to day. Naturally the device failed. The Bartlett case contained forces far beyond Shannon's control.

Messages began to fly between Washington and Japan and Hawaii. The Assistant Chief of Staff for Intelligence, the Secretary of the Army, the Secretary of Defense all wanted to know the extent of the damage. A team of counterespionage agents in Japan got to work on the investigation. Then Shannon was called to Washington. The Pentagon did not need to hear from Shannon in person about the damages. That could have been done on paper. What worried them was how to handle the difficult commander when the story hit the papers.

Was there time to pack up the whole unit and bury its embarrassing commander before some eager reporter got wind of the story? Probably not. Bartlett would retain a civilian lawyer, and since publicity in these times always was in favor of the defendant and adverse to the Army, the lawyer would leak the story. Pentagon press officials advised the Secretary of Defense to expect the worst: sensational stories with banner headlines like "Spy Turns Peacenik, Sells Out Country" might appear; he might be asked at his press conference what he was doing now that the "traitor problem" had been added to the "deserter problem" and the "draft-dodger problem." The reporters would find out about Sword Island, Lord Shannon, and the 243rd. The Army would simply have to contain the story as best it could.

If such stories appeared, the Secretary of Defense put his mind to their impact on the political election. Pressures would come from both sides. Groups might picket military installations with signs like

LBJ THE TRAITOR, NOT BARTLETT

BARTLETT STANDS FOR HONESTY: JOHNSON STANDS FOR BUTCHERY

WITHDRAW, LBJ, LIKE YOUR FATHER SHOULD HAVE DONE

These might provoke brawls with counter groups hefting signs reading

TRAITORS SHOULD BE HUNG

BLACK JUSTICE FOR TRAITOR BARTLETT

BARTLETT'S DOUBLECROSS THREATENS HAWAII. BOMB PEKING NOW

SCREW BARTLETT

Emphatic essayists would muse about "The Mind of Bartlett," writing movingly about the struggles and traumas of modern youth in an amorphous war. Sound thinkers would reason that while Bartlett's case said much about modern youth, society could not condone treason and had to have strict rules for difficult times. And finally, the Army would have to cope with the impact of the case on the morale of the fighting men in Vietnam.

In April, 1968, one month after a beaten and bruised Bartlett was turned over to the Army by the Japanese police, the case came to the attention of the President. The compromise, of course, was not of such importance that it affected "national security." The 243rd had never done much one way or another to affect national security. It was a political adviser who told the President of the affair. The case could dramatize the Administration's lack of moral leadership for the nation's youth and ambiguous moral position in Vietnam. The President instructed the Secretary of Defense to schedule the trial for the week of the Democratic Convention, thus smothering the case with news from Chicago. He also issued instructions that Col. Shannon be transferred to a desk job in the Pentagon and barred from contact with the press. Concerning the court-martial, the Secretary of Defense was directed to gather a panel of officers who were intellectually sound and not given to inflammatory statements about treason. Finally, the President directed that the verdict of the court-martial be firm but not harsh.

In Hawaii, under guard at the Schofield Barracks BOQ, Capt. Bartlett set his defense in motion. He discussed no details of his case with Army investigators, except a legal officer who explained his rights and the charges being prepared against him. And then he prepared himself for a call to his parents that he almost wished the authorities had not allowed him. His parents would be so hurt. They wouldn't understand the role their upbringing had played in this disaster. Bartlett smiled faintly as he thought of the old skull sessions with his father. The Scotsman felt that young men should learn to question social values at puberty, to dissect career alternatives at adolescence, to articulate a well-charted course of life by voting age. How he used to scare childhood friends! At decisiontime father and son went into lengthy sessions of self-examination in which the pros and cons of each possible course of action were exhaustively analyzed. When occasionally the sessions did not bear fruit, the stern, imposing man would say, "Life will not bear all this analysis. We can't anticipate the element of accident," and the discussion would lapse until the following evening. But the element of accident had not been in Bartlett's favor.

"Hello, dad, can you hear me all right?"

"Yes, son. We can hear you fine. Your mother is on the other line."

"Hi, mom."

"Hello, Jonnie." There seemed to be a slight quaver in her voice.

"You got my telegram."

"Yes, Jon, we got it," his father's voice came back. "I've talked with Lew Fulton, the lawyer at the plant. He's given me some names of possible defense attorneys. I've been turned down by several of them already, but there are a number left. There seems to be some question of whether they'll allow you civilian counsel."

"Yeah, I know. They've assigned me a young captain from the Judge Advocate's office. He's OK, but I'd like to get some civilian help. I don't know who this guy reports to."

"I'll keep trying. You can be sure I'll do everything in my power to help, son."

"You've always been good in a crisis, dad, I'll say that. And this is a full-blown crisis. Has there been anything in the papers?"

"Nothing yet."

"Well, I guess you better brace yourself for some notoriety." There was almost a hopeful note in Bartlett's tone.

"Oh, well," his father replied, "that's one of our lesser worries."

"Jon, dear, how are they treating you?" his mother's tremulous voice broke in.

"It's OK, mom. They've got me in a little stuffy room. That's all. It could have been the catacombs, you know."

"Is there anything I can send you?"

"No thanks, mom. Nothing. They probably wouldn't pass it through anyway. Oh, have you heard anything about Maria?"

There was a pause on the other end.

"Hello, mom, are you still there?"

"Yes, son, we're still here."

"I was asking if you'd heard anything about Maria?"

His father's voice came through this time strong but slow, "Yes, Jon, she's back in Cleveland. She's in a hospital here."

"When did she get back? Is she all right!"

"She got back a week ago. You know she was in a Japanese hospital for two weeks."

"No, I didn't know. I lost track. I haven't had time . . . They had me . . . *IS SHE ALL RIGHT!*" Bartlett's voice shouted the last sentence into the phone.

Again there was a pause before his father's voice came across the transoceanic wire.

"They don't know yet, Jon. She'll be in bandages for another month or so . . ."

"And then?"

"And then she's going to have an operation. You see, her cheek and nose were very badly cut . . ."

"I know that. I was the one who policed her up off the street, for God's sake!"

"Calm yourself, Jon. I know it's hard. But they're bringing in a plastic surgeon from New York—the best in the business I'm told . . ."

"You mean they're going to make her over. No, they can't do that. They can't change her."

"Jon. Jon. Get hold of yourself. They're not going to change Maria. They couldn't change her. You know that. No, you must understand that a surgeon can work only with the person's own tissue. There's a whole science of reconstructive surgery."

"Reconstructive . . . How can they possibly do that on the face?"

"If you really want to know I'll tell you. Perhaps you should know what she will go through."

"Tell me, dad. Please, you must tell me."

"Well, the doctor will do a skin graft. From her inner arm to her face. It means . . . it means, Jon, that she'll have her arm strapped across her face for a month. She'll only be able to see out of one eye until they see if the graft takes. But believe me, son, the doctor is the best. I'm sure she'll be all right... eventually."

Later that day an astonishing thing happened that pulled Bartlett out of his near total distraction over the news about Maria, and yanked his thoughts back in his own problems. Word came that Col. Dean Shannon had ordered Capt. Bartlett brought to the 243rd on Sword Island. Bartlett knew the order was illegal and that he could refuse if he wished. Yet a weird curiosity came over him. Why not see what effect the disclosure had had on the old man? What did it matter anyway? Besides, if this illegal order was revealed at the trial, it could go in his favor.

Promptly at 0800 the following morning, three MPs arrived at the BOQ where Bartlett was being confined and escorted him to an Army sedan. Twenty minutes later they pulled up behind a line of cars. Ahead of them the sign read "SWORD ISLAND FERRY." In the middle of the inlet the rusty, prewar ferry labored toward the landing. It gave no impression of motion, but if one looked away for a few minutes and then back at it, it was apparent that some progress had been made. The ferry was an inefficient lifeline for the island. The Navy would not permit a bridge. They were afraid a bridge might impede the ships' escape in any future Pearl Harbors.

When the sedan finally rolled onto the ferry, Bartlett's tension began to develop. The heavy metallic thumping of the engines as they waited to pull out into Pearl pressed in on Bartlett, surrounded him, mocking the throb in his head and the quickened beat of his heart. It knew, even this wise old ferry knew. Bartlett thought he would choke on the sickly sweet smell of gasoline, wet and slick, on the iron slats. Slowly the machine pulled out into the polluted harbor, the gasoline stench mingling with the half-salt, half-sewage dankness of the morning air. One time, Bartlett remembered, after a tropical rain, the old ferry had steered around a pinball machine bobbing in the harbor. It had enlivened the conversation on the morning ride that day. Now around his sedan, Capt. Bartlett listened as GIs conversed about downtown Honolulu and the number of days they had left in service—cannon fodder talk.

It was as if Col. Shannon had planned this ferry ride to impress his workers with the seriousness of their mission. Submarines and destroyers and aircraft carriers slipped noiselessly in and out of the harbor in traffic on their endless adventures on the high seas. Sleek harbor craft cut their way through the harbor, aft cabins decorated with delicately embroidered and tasseled white curtains in the windows, and upholstered in masculine brown leather. They spirited high-ranking officers with scowling expressions away to important conferences, though admittedly the boats sometimes carried these same officers' children and wives to their picnics—on a discreet basis, of course.

But the hulks of rusty steel that protruded unexpectedly from the slimy harbor water showed Shannon's special talent for the dramatic. These were what remained of the *Utah* and the *Arizona,* two of the eight giant battleships sunk during the Japanese sneak attack on Pearl Harbor. Two thousand American sailors died in that attack. For, in its most romantic sense, the mission of the 243rd was to eliminate the element of surprise from any potential enemy in the Far East. That the perimeter of American security had been extended to Vietnam, Thailand, Laos, and other remote areas of the Orient mattered little to the military task. The requirement remained: to know in advance when and in what strength the enemy would attack, whether the attack came at Pearl Harbor or at Udorn Airbase in Thailand. The rusting masses of the *Arizona* and the *Utah* were lasting reminders of an early warning job poorly done.

Business was as usual that morning. A number of destroyers, a troop ship, an ammunition ship, and a cargo vessel were in. Bartlett could make out a disciplined formation of marines on the dock below the troop ship, standing straight, like bullets in a box, waiting to be loaded. He turned away to the destroyers. The sailors said that the return to Pearl from the West Pacific was vital for these World War II destroyers. So much firing off the Vietnam coast shook their screws loose. Handles and turn wheels began to fall off. The ships looked quite harmless, almost impotent in the morning glow. More powerful in appearance were the giant repair cranes behind, looming like prehistoric praying mantises over the assemblage of gray, battle-weary ships.

The ferry chugged on, looking stupid and out of place. Around the bow of the cargo ship, its load came into view. A white, protective chemical coated the Skyraiders. Perhaps they were pupas, Bartlett thought, and became war planes only when transported into the proper environment for hatching. Perhaps they will park that one in front of a Vietnam commander's shack late on the eve of his birthday and tie a big red ribbon on it. "Happy Birthday, Jack. Many happy returns." Not to be so cynical. These planes might have saved Rolland.

Bartlett could make out a swabbie on the dock below the cargo ship. A gray duffel bag lay crumpled at his feet; he was yelling something up to someone on board. He's probably coming off leave, Bartlett thought. Poor bastard. Even swabbies were human in times like these. On duty for long periods soldiers and sailors are bland and uninteresting—their senses dulled by routine and noise. But coming back from leave—rejuvenated by the rediscovery of a world of nice people and human respect, and dreading the return to the grind—this is the low point. Of course, it occurred to Bartlett, he could have been rolled in downtown Honolulu.

Ten minutes later, the sedan stopped in front of the astonishing building that housed the 243rd. The structure had been used for airplane-engine testing during World War II. It was shaped like a hotel in a monopoly game except for two square turrets on either end where the engines had been hoisted in and secured. It had no windows. Iron reinforced rods protruded from the turrets a distance of three or four meters like Gallic fortifications, though no one seemed to know what their purpose had been. An impeccable lawn with small palm trees and orchid beds adorned the blockhouse. Shannon's formula was clear. Discourage generals from dropping in by the island location. When they came, let them be awed by the prideful, spooky appearance. When they asked questions, be discreet. Even generals did not always have a need to know about such sensitive matters. And so majors were given a text of briefing which they read to visiting dignitaries, and were instructed not to be drawn into details. The rest Shannon felt he could handle with the force of his personality.

"Sergeant, here's your prisoner." The escort spoke to an unseen figure behind a steel bar gate that served as the entrance to the building.

"Right, sir," came the answer from nowhere. A buzzer sounded and the gate opened. Someone beckoned to Bartlett to follow him down a long cinder-block corridor, dimly lit at the end by a single florescent tube.

News of Bartlett's arrival had raced through headquarters. Now as he followed his escort down the long corridor, faces appeared in the shadows of the doorways, straining for a glimpse of this pleasant villain they had known and who now jeopardized their livelihood. Bartlett recognized them but uttered nothing in greeting. Sam Kawazaki, Johnny Wong, Joe Limsong, the men who translated or wrote messages or gathered Shannon's statistics. They were the small-minded bureaucrats, retired officers on the lam, naturalized Orientals with a good thing, timid unimaginative men cowering before this bogey of a colonel. They had long since given up on the requirements from the Pentagon. Their problems were more mundane: how to keep up the number of reports coming in from the field each month. One-line reports on fog over Peking were as good as a ten-page on an A-bomb test at Lop Nor. You got just as much credit. The old man demanded three hundred reports on China a month. He would have his three hundred or heads would roll. Statistics not quality would make or break Brigadier General Shannon.

Jack Sujone. Tom Pak. Jerry Shih. They must have been disturbed if they stirred from their cubicles. Their faces reflected awe more than hate. The Bartlett case was beyond their comprehension, thus beyond hatred. They were supposed to be experts in compromise, but none of their training seemed to apply. If an operation were exposed, the finger must point to someone else, or at least provide no conclusive undeniable proof of U.S. involvement. That was the first principle of the game. That was why you had Allies and joint operations, so as to have a fall guy. Since relationships between Americans and Asians are always subtle, these faces in the door always had a convenient excuse for failure. The counterpart had been unprofessional. But how were they going to cover their tracks now.

Nothing in the colonel's outer office had changed. The drab green walls, the pictures of former commanders of the 243rd, a few of whom had also been disgraced, the pictures of the men who made up the chain of command from the President down to Shannon—all dusted and immaculate.

Sgt. Maj. Donahue nodded in recognition as Bartlett entered his office. There was embarrassment on the salty old professional's face. They had joked together so often before.

"The colonel will see you in a few minutes," Donahue said. The "sir" at the end of the sentence was conspicuously absent. Bartlett shifted uncomfortably. He scanned the bulletin board: detail roster, mess hall menus, daily bulletins about social gatherings at the Officers Club. Nothing very interesting except maybe an Easter message to the men:

> In this solemn season of contemplation may we glorify Him who has made everything possible. I pray that we may sanctify His Holy Name through a job well done.
>
> D. Shannon
> Commanding

"The colonel will see you now," Donahue announced as he stepped out of the inner office.

Bartlett clenched his teeth and started toward the interrogation room. He entered the undistinguished soundproof office. To his surprise—Shannon if anything was always good for surprises—behind the bald colonel sat the entire complement of officers in the 243rd. This was to be a board of inquisitors, not just one.

Shannon's team sat erect and self-righteous behind him. Bartlett scanned the group with a flicker of his eyes.

Lt. Col. Pelsey sat on Shannon's right and next to him sat Capt. Dalton. The presence of these two officers astonished Capt. Bartlett beyond his almost total astonishment at Shannon's group staging. These were men whom he liked and respected, who had helped him, and placed confidence in him, and now he had ruined them.

Bartlett did not care about the rest of the club.

Next to Dalton was Maj. Boermann, who had made a reputation for himself in Vietnam by planting a flag with a boar's head on the front of his jeep and driving around Ban me Thout as if he owned it. He greeted people in the morning with a toothy grin, and a thumbs up "Kill VC," and claimed to have a lot of contacts in Vietnam. But among the professionals he was known as a coward, whatever that meant. The others in the group were colorless professionals.

No, Bartlett was just as happy to be on the opposing side of these men, but Pelsey and Dalton . . .

Capt. Bartlett saluted Col. Shannon.

"Sir, Captain Bartlett reports."

The old man sat on the edge of his black leather chair, intent in his last hours in command. Bartlett stood at attention, eyes straight ahead, and waited for the command, "at ease." It did not come.

"*Captain* Bartlett, eh? Oh, that's right, I promoted you, didn't I?"

"Yes, sir."

"Colonel Pelsey wrote such glowing recommendations

after your coup in Taiwan. He put a lot of stock in your abilities, didn't he?"

"Yes, sir, I guess he did."

"You don't need to guess. Colonel Pelsey, you put a lot of faith in Private Bartlett here, didn't you?"

"Yes, sir, I did."

"What about it, Dalton?"

"Yes, sir, the unit in Japan thought highly of Captain Bartlett." Dalton answered in a clear unashamed voice. Two of his operations compromised in the affair, Dalton was not on Bartlett's side.

"How about his professional performance, Major Boermann? You watched his development."

"Well, sir. Major Randsom rated him good operationally and fair in military demeanor. . . ."

"Is that so? I guess I'll have to take your word for it. No point in bothering Stocky in Coeur d'Alene now." And then turning back to Bartlett. "Major Randsom retired a month ago, you see . . . And Lt. Col. Pelsey? What did he say?"

"Lieutenant Colonel Pelsey rated him excellent operationally, good in demeanor."

"Good in military demeanor, eh? Well, I guess we'll all have to pay for Lieutenant Colonel Pelsey's poor judgment now. What about his appearance today, Captain Nerf?"

"His bearing is adequate today, sir."

"Major Holliwell, did you ever sense there was a traitor in Bartlett?" The colonel's voice contained a note of cheerful inquisitiveness.

"He was always a little mysterious, sir. I was always a little suspicious."

"That's your job, goddamn it." The quip betrayed Shannon's irritation for the first time, but he quickly returned to his pleasant tone of curiosity.

"Now then, Bartlett, you must feel a little funny saluting me like you did at first. Do you know what a salute means?"

"Yes, sir."

"What?"

"The book says the hand salute is the outward sign of respect for authority by men under arms."

"Is that right, Lieutenant Perch?"

"Yes, sir." His voice cracked. Lt. Perch was nineteen years old and evidently as scared by this performance as Bartlett.

"You were always good with the book, weren't you, George. And why do you think authority needs to be respected in the Army?"

A wave of overpowering fatigue swept over the young officer. "Because, sir, in combat chaos would result if commands were not respected and obeyed."

"Very good, Bartlett. Now when you salute, do you think the authority you're respecting stops with the man you salute?"

Bartlett's eyes flickered as he struggled to maintain his military bearing and his sanity.

"No, sir, the respect extends up the chain of command to the President of the United States and to the Articles of the Constitution which you are here violating, to the Declaration of Independence which this country and this President are now betraying in Vietnam and . . ."

Shannon's fist came slamming down on his desk. A miniature Civil War cannon which he kept for a paperweight jumped an inch and rolled off the desk. It hit the tile floor with a clang, a wheel broke off and rolled under the sofa. None of the officers moved a finger.

"You dare to be impertinent when you have committed treason against the flag, the President, the Constitution, the military code of conduct and every other goddamned document that this country stands for. Don't throw your hippie arguments out to me, boy. They'll be no help to you when they string you up as a wartime traitor."

The veins in the colonel's bald head became prominent and his dull eyes watered with rage. Not that Bartlett noticed. The display scared him to the very limit of his wits. He awaited the next barrage, his belly knotted in terror.

Colonel Shannon tried to compose himself. His hands trembled as he began again in a low tone, "Bartlett, you have succeeed in destroying the 243rd and every man in it. You may be proud of that if you wish. What is more important, you have set back military intelligence in the Far East ten years, and at a time when it is as critical as the year when the Japs bombed those hulks of steel you saw from the ferry. If the Chicoms enter the Vietnamese war in a surprise attack, we may not be ready now. Your highmindedness has dried up the Army's capability to warn our troops beforehand. Just from the humanitarian side of it"—Shannon mocked the word—"you may be responsible for the death of thousands of American GIs. I hope to God there's someone else who can fill the vacuum.

"Our mission here in relation to China or Burma or Thailand or North Korea, your mission with Y-140, the mission of Pelsey's and Dalton's operations which you sabotaged—all were justified by military necessity. Check back into any document you like—the Nuremburg Trials, the Tokyo Trials, the Kellogg-Briand Pact, the Geneva Accords, the damn Hague Rules of Land Warfare—the right of acting on military necessity is justified on moral grounds."

Shannon grimaced. "You didn't think we career people could read, did you, George? *NOW GET OUT OF HERE!*"

Salutes were exchanged. Bartlett did an about-face and walked out of the office.

The victor shall not be asked later whether we were telling the truth or not. In starting and making a war, not the right is what matters, but victory.

—ADOLPH HITLER

May 10. Back in his drab chamber of detention, Captain Bartlett was hot and feverish. He was still shaken from his meeting with Col. Shannon. Beneath his proper well-starched facade he felt he had been living on the brink of madness for months, as if he were jailed in some inescapable sound chamber with overly loud Wagnerian music pelting him from every side. He cursed himself now for his stupid outburst before Shannon. How could he have been so childish? He had justified every thought of naivete that the officers had about him. Those ninnies. Pelsey and Dalton were really no different. When had they ever a thought about the ethics of power? Most of them never read a newspaper. The only morality that ever concerned them was what to do with a hapless private who knocked up a girl.

Capt. Bartlett paced the thirty feet of his green linoleum floor. Was there no end to this torment? He stopped in front of a painting that hung over his bunk. "Breakthrough at Chipyong-ni" it was entitled. Clever that they should have put a propaganda painting in his room. He read the inscription: "In February, 1951, the 23rd Infantry Combat Team with attached

Dutch and French units was cut off and surrounded by an overwhelming force of Chinese Reds in the narrow valley of Chipyong-ni." The youth studied the distorted, gnarled face of the GI yelling back for more ammunition. The artist had painted the face in blue to accentuate the horrible pressure of the Red attack. The hordes of Chinese rushing the American position occupied only a small portion of the lower left-hand corner. The mass of formless Chinese was painted in light brown brightened by the yellow of an artillery blast.

The artist had performed his commission well. Here was the classic view of war in Asia—the individual American GI fighting and dying for freedom against the swarm of slant-eyed Communists. What kind of painting would the Pentagon come up with about Vietnam when it was all over? Surely they would not paint the American adviser standing by, helpless though shocked, as his Vietnamese counterpart tortured a Vietcong with the water treatment.

Perhaps the MPs had missed an opportunity, he thought. Instead of this propaganda picture, they could have put up an oriental scroll to remind the prisoner of the people he had destroyed. Chuang's graceful motions across the ricepaper during training in Kaohsiung. Maria's tasteful, tatami living room in Asakusa. Maria! Where are you now! In some colorless, sterile hospital room. At least this time you are in the hands of certified doctors!

Bartlett took up his pacing again. If only he had been placed in a regular military stockade. There he would have had others to divert him. Even a cold dungeon deep below some ammunition dump would be better than this light olive-drab room. After all, he deserved a dungeon. He was a traitor, wasn't he? He demanded to be treated like one. He insisted on being interrogated by some scar-faced inquisitor with a shaved head and a starched uniform that creaked with every movement. He wanted to be shown by brutal logic how he had been led into political divergencies, and induced without torture to sign a confession of complicity with the opposition.

That would not happen in the American Army, Bartlett knew that. Some scrubbed crew-cut youth with two years of college and three months of Army investigative training would gather the facts. He would search out Bartlett's friends and ask the stock questions. Did the interviewee know Capt. Bartlett socially? Did he drink excessively? Had he ever taken drugs? Was he emotionally stable? Did the interviewee ever have political discussions with Bartlett? Did Bartlett ever express any disaffection with American policy in Vietnam? Did the interviewee have any reason to doubt Capt. Bartlett's loyalty to the United States? The answers would be plugged into the proper boxes on the Army investigation form, the evidence would be presented at the trial, he would be proven undramatically guilty of treason under the Uniform Code of Military Justice, and that would be the end of it.

Did he deserve anything different? The captain ran his fingers through his tousled hair. How could the law make an exception for naive transgressors? The damage to American interests was the same. What credence could a plea of justifiable disloyalty have in times like these? To think that he had entertained the notion that he was removing the provocative power of the United States in the Far East with his letters! In times of dubious international policy, could the law be any less absolute toward idealistic violators? What did it mean for him, Capt. Bartlett, U.S. Army, to plead that he had acted from a higher law? Oh, God, was it possible that he had ruined his life for an idea that did not exist?

The soldier flopped his frame on the stark bunk. It was so bright in the room. He rubbed his eyes and then his arm came across his face. That kept out the light. Could he doze? Not very likely. Too many things to think about. Perhaps if he tried the Yoga technique of consciously relaxing every muscle. First the toes, then the ankles, then the calfs. Breathe deeply. It was dark enough with his arm across his eyes. But how would he relax his arm muscles in that position? It was uncomfortable. And then his eyes opened wide, and he stared at the ceiling. His arm adjusted itself so that he could only see out of one eye. He pressed the arm tight against his face. He moved it around a little and tried to think what it would be like if he couldn't move it. And then he got up and took out a piece of paper.

Dear Maria,

Yesterday I heard the news about your operation. I can't imagine what you are going through, but I know it is worse than my situation. But we will both come through all right. I know we will. I'm going to write to you often, as much as I possibly can in the coming weeks. Some of my letters may not get through because my mail is censored. You don't have to answer them if you don't want to. You don't even have to read them or have them read, if you don't want to. But it means a lot to me to write them. Because I still love you very much. And I want to help. Love,

Jon

The day after the meeting with Col. Shannon the trial date of August 26, 1968, was unobtrusively announced at the end of the U.S. Army Hawaii Daily Bulletin. A Pentagon public information officer was sent to Hawaii exclusively to handle the case.

Several days later, high in Halawa Heights on a promontory overlooking Pearl Harbor, a cocktail party was going on at General George Claremont Strand's house. The white board house was undistinguished from the outside, one of the many low one-story houses in Halawa that sacrifices design for copious window space. But Mrs. Strand, a tall, graceful woman of forty, had arranged the inside with a comfortable elegance. The focus of the living room was a semi-circle of feathery baise couches around the expanse of window which bestowed on the guest a magnificent view of the brilliant sunsets over the Waianae Range. With the thick green carpet and green felt wall covering, with the Japanese scrolls and Thai Buddha figurines, with the prints of Gen. Strand's Afghan hounds, and the photographs of him in the important moments of his career (in shorts on the Burma Road as one of Stillwell's youngest majors, receiving a silver star at Pusan, in battle gear next to a tank somewhere in Florida during the Cuban missile crisis) the room was very pleasant indeed.

The party was in celebration of General Strand's second star and to bid him farewell, perhaps a bit prematurely, for Vietnam. His 12th Infantry Brigade was within a month of completing its training at Schofield Barracks before deployment to Quang Nhai Province. With a successful campaign in Vietnam Strand would be in line for the top. Brass in Hawaii already rumored that he would be the Army Chief of Staff one day.

Strand was a model general. He stood six-feet-four and had a lean, athletic look to him. He kept his silver hair closely cropped now, and in uniform his appearance and his dignity could inspire the most hardened anti-militarist. On this occasion he was also a model host, relaxed and attentive, moving comfortably from a discussion of a forthcoming presidential visit with Admiral Robert E. Lee Edge, the Commander in Chief of the Pacific, to the small talk of schools and assignments with the younger officers.

Midway through the party General Strand noticed J. A. Kilpatrick, the publisher of the Honolulu *Star* and *Telegram*, standing on the fringe of a coterie around Admiral Edge. Though no milquetoast, Kilpatrick was flattered by invitations from powerful men and justified going to these parties by the need to keep up good relations with his paper's military clientele. Strand moved to him.

"Hello, J.A. I'm glad you could come. How's your drink?"

"Well, thank you, General. Oh, I'm fine," Kilpatrick said, trying to stand his straightest, as he looked up at the general, "Congratulations on the new star. I wish you many more."

"Gettin' too old for any more than another three, J.A."

Both men enjoyed a hearty laugh.

"How's the brigade look?"

"Couldn't be better, thanks. We've put these boys through the toughest training we know how. They've done beautifully. Morale is good, real good."

"I'm happy to hear that, General. I wish you all the best of luck over there."

"Thank you, sir. We'll do fine."

"You know, General, the different impressions that one gets of this younger generation never cease to amaze me. On the one hand, you hear of soldiers like yours making sacrifices for their country, sometimes the supreme sacrifice, with not so much as a complaint; and then you read about the hippies evading the draft, taking drugs, lying in the streets. It's an amazing time."

"Well, I don't know about the others, J.A., but if you could work with my boys for a while, knowing what they are preparing themselves for, you'd see where the idealism is nowadays."

"But, don't you think some of the college kids have idealism too, General? I mean, I'm sure you must know there are some sincere protesters in the country."

"Well, they're not my concern, J.A."

"Has anyone in the 12th Brigade ever refused to do his military duty for anti-Vietnam feelings?"

"Are you kidding? The troops know we'd hang anyone who tried. Look, when you ready a brigade for combat, you concentrate on one thing: survival. You hammer into these numbskulls that the tougher and more aggressive they are, the better their chance to make it is. That's true, and it works. These kids are too tired and too worried about their own skins to get political."

"But what about the smarter kids who are already political?"

"No difference. Second thoughts are too dangerous in combat. Once that's understood, you don't have trouble. People are much like sheep, you know."

Kilpatrick nodded, a little shocked and a little thrilled at the same time.

"Tell me this, General. When do you think all the killing will stop?"

General Stran grimaced, and looked away to other guests. "How should I know, J.A.? That's not my business."

Kilpatrick decided he was pushing things, and changed the subject.

"I've been admiring your dog prints, General. What kind of dog is this?"

"Afghan hound. I've been breeding them for fifteen years."

"Very interesting. They're lovely things."

"Do you know anything about dogs?"

"Beyond our cocker's taste for my slippers, no."

"Well, the Afghan is a sight hound. That means he stalks his prey by seeing it and then giving chase, rather than by smelling it. Over rough terrain and long distances there's no finer hunter in the world."

"The ones in your prints sure don't look like hunters, unless they hunt blue ribbons."

"The long coat has been bred into 'em for beauty, J.A. The real hunters in Afghanistan or in ancient Egypt have a shorter coat. It's true of dogs in general, that the ones raised in uncivilized areas are closer to the original breed. Their masters don't always feed them their Alpo on schedule, so they have to kill to eat occasionally. You know, living by the law of nature."

"Fascinating."

"Have you ever read Charles Darwin?"

Kilpatrick nodded his head. "Some," he said.

"Well, he talks about what civilization does to breeds. He says the ears of domesticated dogs droop because the ear muscles aren't used much. The dog is seldom alarmed. Also the molar structure changes."

"I suppose that means human ears will droop someday."

"Except the human animal perks up his ears to other things like gossip. But you're right, our ears do have to be trained to danger. We find, for instance, that mountain boys or Indians make our best point-men on small patrols."

"A special breed of men, huh?"

"You should see 'em work, J.A."

"I'd like to."

"I'll arrange it. . . . Say, would you like to have a look at my dogs? It'd just take a minute."

Kilpartick followed the general through the jovial crowd and out into the yard.

The two men stood admiring the regal angular dogs for a time, as Kilpatrick heard more about the breed and its stages of development. The general let one of the fluffy puppies out, and it jumped and nuzzled around Kilpatrick.

"I still can't imagine them as hunters," Kilpatrick said.

The general smiled, and then returned the dog to its cage.

"J.A., going back to what we were talking about first, you

know it's not in the combat troops that you're going to find the troublemakers. It's the support troops—the crowd that sits on the sidelines and cries about how awful it all is. Did you know that for every gun carrier in the U.S. Army there's ten support troops? No other Army in the world operates on that basis."

"Are you thinking about those four sailors who defected to the Communists from that carrier. What was it, the *Enterprise?*

"Exactly. Their chief probably told 'em to polish a brass bell over again, and they ran off to Russia saying they didn't want to participate in America's capitalist imperialist war any more."

"That reminds me, general, what about the case of this captain you're putting on trial for treason?"

"Bartlett? I'm glad you mentioned that, J.A. I'm on the investigative board. You know, there's one major difference between training men and training dogs: the morale factor. That's my concern as I get my men ready for combat. And I'll be frank with you, that case could hurt the morale of the brigade. As you know, our deployment to Vietnam just about coincides with the Bartlett trial. It's not going to be good if there's a lot of talk around about treason and 'moral dilemmas.' I can't tell you how to run your newspapers, J.A. but I hope you'll keep that in mind before you sensationalize this case."

"How's the Army going to handle it?"

"As tight-lipped as possible. We've barred him from civilian counsel for security reasons. I argued that no information whatever be allowed out, but I was overruled by the Department of the Army. They're so damned concerned about being democratic nowadays. . . . Oh, this is off the record, by the way."

"Sure."

"Well, if they insist on making the trial public, they sure as hell better nail his pelt to the wall. Otherwise, we're going to have little 'moral dilemmas' crawling all over the place."

The general could not tell if he had impressed his point on Kilpatrick. The newspaperman maintained his thoughtful, noncommittal look. General Strand leaned toward him for the clincher.

"If you had a son in the Army now, J.A., you'd understand what I mean."

The following day, J. A. Kilpatrick, who controlled all news outlet in Hawaii, announced at an editorial meeting that the Bartlett case would be downplayed. The reason given was management's fear of alienating the military readership of the two papers: over fifty percent of the subscriptions. The chain's military expert, a former captain in the Marines, was instructed to watch for a verdict and print it in a paragraph on the back page.

Jon, *July 29, 1968*

News from Skinny Minnie today: Shige got 10 years. Takahashi now in charge of Kakumaru

M.

In both cases the emotional commitment came first; the arguments later. This may seem like a humiliating confession for a political writer to make. How can anybody value the judgment and trust the critical faculties of a person whose political allegiances were derived, by his own admission, from such absurd sentimental experiences? . . .

Political maturity does not, alas, coincide with age. Many conversions at an adult age, whether religious or political are the result of an immature psychological make-up, and differ only little from the primary infantile process of acquiring a faith.

—ARTHUR KOESTLER, Arrow in the Blue

August 24. Somewhere on the huge Army training base at Schofield Barracks, Hawaii, on a narrow byway named, with that particular Army flair, Artillery Road, a small wooden building stands out in peculiar dissimilarity to the long, flat, blockish structures around it. The high pointed roof, the tall narrow windows, the small steps in front of the building projected the certain quaintness of a one-room schoolhouse. With a small bell on its roof, the structure could have been George Washington's schoolhouse at Mount Vernon. It is, however, the military courtroom.

If the exterior of the court appears unjudicial in the extreme, the inside as well makes no pretensions to being a hallowed hall of justice. Folding chairs are arranged neatly in rows. Several scuffed tables and lecterns stand in haphazard juxtaposition for the convenience of the defense and prosecution. And raised on the dais, made of freshly varnished plywood, the bench dominates the room. The semicircular judgment seat can accommodate ten officers for a full-dress general court-martial, though normally the court went into session as a summary court with only one officer acting as judge and jury, rarely as executioner. In the case of the United States Army vs. Capt. Jonathan Bartlett, nine officers would comprise the general court.

Around the walls of this cheerless structure, in between the windows that provided light and some distraction in the long cases, picture posters depicting the six articles of the United States Army Code of Conduct hang as a reminder of the solemn purposes for which an Army exists. All offered the familiar visage of the idealistic American soldier sustained in battle by the misty image of his home, his church, and his flag. It is an art form which Communist countries carry to the greatest heights and which the American Army does very poorly. Hovering benevolently or malevolently (depending on your point of view) over the defense table is the sixth of the articles:

> I will never forget that I am an American fighting man, responsible for my actions, and dedicated to the principles which made my country free. I will trust in my God and in the United States of America.

At the break of dawn on the morning of August 26th, a detail of privates set about making the small building ready for trial. MPs were stationed outside at 0700 hours. Their orders were to allow only authorized personnel into the building. This was to be an executive session in which classified matters would be discussed, therefore there would be no audience. For the defendant it would be a particularly discomforting situation. Surrounded by the immutable tenets of military law, without the possible comfort of an impartial audience behind him, without the presence of a press who might see beyond the military details of his case, a naked captain would face a board of nine field-grade officers in an empty courtroom.

At 0830 hours Capt. Bartlett was dressed and ready for his escort. He looked at himself in the mirror for a final inspection. His hair was freshly cut, his shoes and brass polished, his uniform well-starched. His gaze fell on a tuft of chest hair that peeked out from the V collar of his khaki shirt, and then lowered to the bulge in his pants. Bartlett knew that the starched shirt would rub his nipples sore and red by the end of the day. It was the price of looking "strack." But he wanted to look the part of the well-healed soldier that day. He would not offer his accusers the joy of feeling that they were rooting out a misfit.

The Hawaiian sun was bright and warm that morning. Mountainous tropical clouds moved across the blue sky, forming what Bartlett had thought as a child was a world of infinite bounciness where children could hop from rubbery knoll to rubbery knoll, slow-motion, spring to the peaks, and then fall gently over backwards in endless somersaults, giggling all the way down. The soldier raised his pale face to the sky as he was guided toward the waiting MP car. The spiny fronds of the royal palms on Artillery Road slapped against one another in the gentle wind, and an amusing myna bird hopped purposefully over the lawn, well kept by stockade prisoners. Capt.

Bartlett glanced at his shadow on the walkway. He readjusted his garrison cap.

His butterflies began again now. Like a black child in a ghetto, he was in a situation completely beyond his control. And yet he felt he should be grateful that the final, inevitable, contemptible destiny was near. He wondered if all guilty men like himself suffered their worst agony before their guilt was officially proclaimed. These dreadful moments of anxious uncertainty made him unsteady on his feet.

The spectrum of all possible punishments raced through his mind. What if they sentenced him to be hanged? How would he spend his last hours? What would he ask for as a last request? Perhaps a small Filipino cigar and a snifter of Courvoisier. Aw, come on, the MPs would laugh all the way to the hitching post. Maybe he would demand that Maria be brought to him. Would her doctors allow it? If not, he would proclaim his love for her in a flowery speech on the gallows before they put the hood over him. But what if he only went to jail for life? Then at least he could begin to adjust immediately. Adjustment, thank God, was only hours away. His old grandmother used to say in her thick Scottish brogue, "A man can get used to anything but hanging."

A small crowd awaited Capt. Bartlett at the courthouse. A few reporters from the wire services were there as well as a photographer from the Honolulu *Telegram* to take pictures for their files. The *Telegram*'s military expert had been called away to Chicago. One of the reporters yelled a few questions at Bartlett as the MPs hustled him into the building.

"What are ya going to plead, Cap'n?"

"Is it going to be a long trial?"

"Are you a traitor, Captain?"

With an embarrassed smile Bartlett shrugged his shoulders noncommittally and entered the courthouse.

The commotion outside contrasted with the near emptiness and quiet of the chamber. The two prosecutors huddled on some technicality which bore on the presentation of their sturdy case. They glanced up as Bartlett entered, and then back to one another as if they had not seen him. Bartlett's defense counsel, poor man, sat alone. The judges had not arrived.

The defendant exchanged a few words with his counsel, an eager young captain from Harvard, and glanced over to the stack of incriminating evidence on the prosecutor's desk. The prosecutor was carefully arranging his folders in neat piles. Bartlett hoped that the prosecution had all the facts right. And then his eyes raised to the poster over him:

> I am an American fighting man, responsible for my actions and dedicated to the principals which made my country free. I will trust in my God and in the United States of America.

The dictum was difficult to adapt to the Vietnam war and to Chuang. His responsibility to his God, to his view of the principles which made his country free, and to military authority did not coincide. Each responsibility—religious, political, military—seemed to pull him in different directions like some ancient Roman horse torture reserved for the worst criminals. If these pulls on him contradicted one another, what then was the primary responsibility? The military responsibility? Was he not vain to think otherwise—that he could make his own rules?

These thoughts had gnawed on Capt. Bartlett in the months of his detention. It was difficult to work out an answer without help, but the system offered only clichés and continuing warfare.

When, in the week before his trial, in pacing back and forth under the picture of Chipyong-ni, Bartlett decided his actions had been wrong, he breathed a deep sigh of relief. Above all he wanted a release from doubt, an end to analysis.

The solution did not come in a flash of intuition, perhaps because it was a disappointing undramatic solution. It provided no profound answer to the riddle, no escape from the dilemma. His surrender was personal, not intellectual.

Why had he become involved in the first place? Bartlett dug back into the murky events that led up to his induction. Snatches of memory came back to him. Teaching elementary school . . . Chinese art . . . Maria . . . tutoring in Japanese and Chinese . . . it had been a happy period in Cleveland. Why had he given it up? Bartlett tried to think.

What had been his view of the war then? Could he have been swayed by the argumentation of those days? Only the horrible things stuck in his mind . . . homeless families . . . pot-holed fields . . . "freedom-loving peasants of South Vietnam" . . . "struggle for the hearts and minds of the people." Perhaps it had been a desire to be relevant. That was more like it. What value did these emotions have in the real world? How could his human anguish be translated into the language of relevant political opinion? Chinese Communism did have to be contained, didn't it? Pulling out of Vietnam would mean a dominolike fall of other Southeast Asian countries, wouldn't it? So how was one to mesh the emotional with the intellectual, the language of human feeling with the language of power politics? What relevance did his emotions have to the torment of the decisionmaker? What was his alternative global strategy?

Had his confusion on these points been enough to propel him into the service? Surely not. Even with Vietnam there had still been talk of eliminating the draft in 1965. Why should he be one of the last suckers?

And then Bartlett remembered. He had listened to the President's speech in the teacher's lounge. Miss Bird was eating one of her banana cream puffs. She had just taken a big chomp when the President shattered the illusion: "This is really war.

It is guided by North Vietnam and it is spurred by Communist China. Its goal is to conquer the South, to defeat American power and to extend the Asiatic dominion of Communism. And there are great stakes in the balance. . . ." Her beady little eyes shot a glance at Bartlett as if she wanted to make a comment. Mr. Davis. Smug Mr. Davis, the fifth-grade English teacher, had turned to him.

"Well," he said, "now your generation has a war to fight."

July 28, 1965. Bartlett's service began September 5. It was not that his country was threatened or simply at war. Rather he had viewed his induction as an act of loyalty to his own generation. Right or wrong his contemporaries were making the sacrifices. His romanticism lay in his desire to protect his humanism from the charge of cowardice or ignorance, or, ironically, naivete. And so he went—partly in curiosity, partly because, he thought at the time, everyone else had to.

His instincts then had been true enough, perhaps even commendable, and his disappointing answer now could accommodate them.

"Tennn—hut!" bellowed the MP's voice from the rear of the court room. Capt. Bartlett instinctively leapt to rigid attention. The nine officers filed down the center aisle and took their place at the table.

"At ease, and be seated, gentlemen," the senior colonel said in a civilized voice. The nine put their briefcases on the table and began to get organized.

Bartlett looked back on his life at twenty-seven. What had it meant? He had had his high moments. In sports, in the classroom, in bed. He was intelligent and well educated. There had been potential there. His mind was keen to the social issues of the day. He had his father to thank for that. But what had his life meant so far? Not much really.

Bartlett had shuffled through some of his papers and notes

from the year past in this detention period, and had come across a page from his journal dated March 28, 1968. It had been written during the awful days of decision in Japan, in his mood of longing for Maria and right before the news of Rolland's death.

It read,

The anxieties of youth—how intense and insoluble they are. The imponderables of innocence lost and maturity not yet gained: the longing for manhood, the yearning for love and for friendship, the gnawing in the night for the smell and sound and touch of a woman. The struggle for direction in life: the first enlightenment, the excitement of ideas, the sensation of belief; the first sense of capability and the rude shock of limitation. And the career. Is it right for me?

As if these problems are not enough, there is the society: it's brutality and beauty, its pronouncements and its acts, its history, its hypocrisy, its excitement, its demise.

And the war: so terrible, so incongruous, so complicated, feeding the worst impulses of Americans. You didn't have to be mature to see that. Their appetite for violence, their bent for simplification, their racism.

How should one approach the spectacle? With what is involvement impossible and with what necessary? What compromises does patriotism demand and what compromises can it not demand? When is innocence humanitarian and maturity brutality, and when the reverse? How to deal with despair? What is the answer?

And what if I say your absolute loyalty is due only to the bumblebee who sucks the hibiscus in the hot noon sun; your involvement shall be only with causes of the poor and victimized, never with the profiteers and vandals of America; that you shall compromise only as your ideals deepen from knowledge of life; and find your sustenance in modest, untarnished pursuits?

Will you be weak or will you be strong? Will you be wise or narrow in the end? Who will be your models besides Thoreau? Will you have a pat answer for the hot steel rolling out of Pittsburg ovens, for the purple, blue, green, blinking faces of dazed humanity on Times Square, for the dam builders, the spacemen, the pioneers, the peacemakers and Franklin Roosevelt? How will your formula accommodate General MacArthur and Hitler, Hollywood and the Grand Tetons?

Synthesis, analysis, dialectics, patchwork—what kind of an approach is that? A philosophy without belief as complex as a society—a philosophy that doesn't tell you how to take the next step forward.

Bartlett had sent the page to Maria, as if to make her understand now when it was too late what he had gone through in Japan. He was not sure the page had passed the censors, until he received back a two-sentence note from her—the kind he had received occasionally during the last four months in response to his torturously long letters to her. Her notes were always short, never written in her handwriting.

Jon,
Too much analysis. The heart is more important.
Maria.

She was right but he could not help the dominance of his mind over his emotion. He might have wished that his emotions did not interfere with his thoughts as much as they did, or vice versa, but then Maria would never have been interested in him. In the end he had concluded that there was no way out of his dilemma, just as there had been no clear imperatives that got him into the fix in the beginning. His answer was simple: the situation had not justified the ruin of five young lives. Now his mistake was irrevocable, just as had been the mistakes of Chuang and Ray Rolland, Shige and Maria.

Now the weary young man desired one final thing. He longed to be shown that his mistake was not even an honorable one. For in his deeper thoughts he clung, like all criminals, to the notion that his society must share the blame for his crime. Had it not been for the decimation of Vietnam, he reasoned, or the exploitation and then slaughter of Rolland and Chuang, or the idealism of Shige and the embitterment of Maria, he might not have acted as he did. Also, had the hopes of his generation not been raised and then dragged down again into a bog of confusion, things might have been different. Could the court not expunge this last vestige of self-satisfaction? It would make it much easier to face the music.

"Captain Bartlett, I will read you Article 31 of the Uniform Code of Military Justice," came a voice from the distance. "No person subject to this article may compel any person to incriminate himself . . ."

We cannot say that a private citizen shall be placed in the position of being compelled to determine in the heat of war whether his government is right or wrong or, if it starts right, when it turns wrong. We would not require the citizen, at the risk of becoming a criminal under the rules of international justice, to decide that his country has become an aggressor and that he must lay aside his patriotism, the loyalty to his homeland, and the defense of his own fireside at the risk of being adjudged guilty of crimes against peace on the one hand, or of becoming a traitor to his country on the other, if he makes an erroneous decision based upon facts of which he has but vague knowledge. To require this of him would be to assign to him a task of decision which the leading statesmen of the world and the learned men of international law have been unable to perform in their search for a precise definition of aggression.

—International Military Tribunal,
Nuremberg; English Record, p. 15706f

In the late winter and early spring of 1968, the Military High Command in Saigon finalized its plans for the invasion of North Vietnam, and the system of gathering battlefield intelligence gained the highest priority. Reconnaissance planes or pilotless drones roared over the invasion zone photographing every square foot of ground. Back in an air-conditioned room in a northern airfield of South Vietnam, skin-headed eighteen-year-olds, trained by the Army in photo interpretation, peered through thick lenses at the photographs. Enemy troop concentrations and gun emplacements popped up as if they were arranged on a scale model beneath the lenses. This information was then fed into a Saigon computer and, once confirmed by satellite photographs, ended up as bombing targets flashed to the Strategic Air Command on Guam or Okinawa, and as data fed into the planning packets of Army and Marine field commanders. It was an awe-inspiring system, and the briefers in Saigon spoke of it off the record as if it lay somewhere between the beautiful and the sublime.

This reliance on electronic gadetry that characterizes the American way of war seemed to take on a life of its own. Electronics became the only language that American commanders could speak. And so, when it came to the key question: What would China do?, the Americans knew only to turn to Taiwan's U-2 flights over Kwangsi and Yunnan Provinces. Their photographs could be translated into the words and symbols of the Saigon computers.

In such a system, even without the Bartlett debacle, there was little place for the 243rd. Even if the unit had produced usable information, it would be difficult to analyze its reliability. It could not be photographed or blown up or three-dimensionalized; it could not be rechecked or systematized or computerized. It just wouldn't fit. Americans are no better at personalized intelligence than they are at personalized war.

"You Americans are too rich, too honest, too moral, and too kind to be successful with Asians," a Japanese gentleman told Bartlett once.

And then shortly after March 31, 1968, the Top Secret invasion plans were downgraded in importance.

Captain Jonathan Bartlett pleaded guilty to all counts including the ones under Article 104 of the Uniform Code of Military Justice about "Aiding the Enemy." He shouldn't have done that because in the Army's desire to make an example of him, some of the charges had been trumped up. But strangely, Bartlett didn't even allow his defense counsel to plead extenuating circumstances. As a result he got three years at Leavenworth, was stripped of his commission, given a dishonorable discharge, and made to forfeit all pay and allowances.

The whole thing was a letdown to the few reporters who had been assigned to the case. The trial lasted only half a day. The two photographers on the story thought the officers were coming out for a lunch break, and didn't even get a picture of Bartlett as he left. They felt stupid afterwards—like Matthew Brady at the Gettysburg Address; he was still setting up his equipment when Lincoln finished.

Bartlett was detained at the Schofield Barracks stockade for two weeks before being shipped to Kansas.

Several days before he left the islands, Lt. Col. Pelsey, for whom the entire case had been catastrophic and beyond comprehension, was jawing with several majors at the Officers Club about the impossibility of Vietnamese-American counterpart relationships, when a young first lieutenant entered the club and sat down next to the lieutenant colonel at the bar. The lieutenant ordered a scotch, and sipped it slowly, mildly interested in the discussion. At a lull in the conversation, he turned to Pelsey and said, "Excuse me, sir, aren't you Lieutenant Colonel Pelsey?"

"That's right."

"I thought I recognized you. I'm Lieutenant Folsom. I'm the officer of the guard for Captain Bartlett, or ex-Captain Bartlett, I should say."

Pelsey was immediately interested. He wanted to know what Bartlett had been doing in the stockade since his sentencing. The lieutenant replied that the prisoner looked out of the window most of the time and wrote a lot of letters. They had a few more drinks. Pelsey described what had happened to the 243rd as result of the affair: How Col. Shannon had been sent to Washington and buried in the Pentagon, how the other officers had been scattered around the world in various intelligence assignments, and how Maj. Jones was handling the final disposition of chairs and desks on Sword Island.

"Funny how all this proved unnecessary, since the trial didn't cause much of a splash anyway," Pelsey concluded, and then offered to buy the lieutenant another drink. The young officer refused and then with a quizzical expression on his face said, "I shouldn't show you this, sir, but I think you'll be interested and maybe you can explain how it fits into the case." He reached into his breast pocket and pulled out several crumpled pieces of paper. "One of my nosey corporals found this in Bartlett's trash can today and brought it to me."

It was a couple of pages of a letter written on a legal pad.

"That's Bartlett's writing all right," Pelsey mumbled. "It looks so stylish and full of character from a distance, but you can hardly read the damn stuff."

Dear Maria,

I can still remember well a Sunday I spent in basic training at Ft. Jackson. It was a crisp Fall day in those sandy South Carolina hills, and I was bundled up in my field jacket and dirty fatigues on my way to the post library. The library was the only place I could relax during those eight weeks. It always used to surprise me that those libraries had pretty fair classical music sections. Not bad on art either. I guess you'd rather not check it out though.

Anyway, I began to hear a loudspeaker in the distance. The Army was very new to me then, and I was curious about everything. So I made for the noise. It turned out that it came from the post chapel. One of those odd majors, the chaplain, was giving his sermon. I couldn't quite figure out why it was blaring out on the loudspeaker because nobody was outside so there must have been seats in the church. Anyhow, much to my surprise, after the usual religious stuff, I heard the words: "You men may well find God in the Army!"

The comment horrified me at the time. If the church had to rely on the killing and the strain of combat for its conversions, what kind of noble recruitment was that? And yet I was always fascinated by the spiritual examination that combat forces on men. I know that's only a masculine fascination. But I wanted to ask a friend of mine, Ray Rolland, that question. He probably could not have answered. He played the odds with Vietnam the way he played them with his ugly girl friends. It was a pretty sure thing. Nobody in our specialty had ever been hurt before.

Oh, Maria, I've had such silly romantic notions about my involvement in this war. I can remember those anguished days of choice in 1965, which you did not appreciate, when I refused the glamorous offers of the Navy and the Air Force to train in some sophisticated weapons system or other. They told me that was where the action was, that I would have a lot more responsibility fast, and I wanted to reply that there would be a lot more moral responsibility too.

No, there was something all wrong about a Capt. Bartlett as the chauffeur of a B-52 bomber, returning to the Officers Club on Guam with tales of heroics in the stratosphere. Somehow that symbolized everything that was wrong with our entanglement over there.

That must have been why I sought out the more personalized side of the war. I know you don't approve, Maria, but let me try to work this out. At least there I could be clear about the consequences of my actions. Later, involved in training an espionage agent called Chuang (you would have loved his sensitivity), it occurred to me that the B-52 job was the lesser evil. Their missions at least were connected with protecting American lives like Rol-

land's. Ironic, isn't it, that one measly operation and one lousy death was too much for me?

Something else bothers me too. In the past three years I gave into all the instincts that made Vietnam possible: militarism, racism, exploitation, sterile theorizing, fascination with power. I guess you realized some of that after my tirade at the Beeto with Shige. You put me through such hell after that, Maria. But it's too bad, because I knew those instincts as evils before I began.

When I ended up going to the opposite extreme, it was partly motivated by Rolland's death in Hue, but more by my need for you. I wanted to hurt my country for using Rolland, for embittering you, for destroying my values. Is that stupid and childish? I don't know. It's so hard to hurt one's country nowadays—almost as hard as it is to help it. The dangerous ones, it appears, are those who want to be helpful. Their letdown is so great. It would have been luckier not to give a damn. Why destroy yourself?

I wonder now if there is still time to salvage our lives. If I were released tomorrow, what could I do? At the moment I am only qualified as a subversive and a saboteur. No doubt I would be in great demand. Perhaps it is just as well that I will be in jail for the next three years. At least I'll be out of the way. Maybe the war will be over then. Wouldn't it be wonderful to be positive again!

We're all victims of this war, Maria, but how can I compare my guilt to your accident or to Rolland's death or to Ch . . .

Oh, Maria, if I could only see you so we could . . ."

The letter trailed off and the last sentence was struck out with bold lines. Pelsey's gaze wandered slowly from the letter.

"Who's this Maria, Colonel?" the young lieutenant asked.

"She's some radical broad that Bartlett got tangled up with in Tokyo."

"And Rolland?"

"Lieutenant Ray Rolland. He was a friend of Bartlett's who got picked off at Hue during Tet."

The lieutenant folded up the wrinkled letter, a quizzical look still on his young face, and put it back in his pocket. Pelsey remained silent for a time.

"Strange," he said finally, "Bartlett told me once what

importance he attached to throwing away a letter when it was not quite appropriate. He considered it a sign of maturity."

MAC Contract Flight B-384, originating in Tan Son Nhut AFB, Saigon, for Travis AFB, California, with intermediate stops at Clark AFB, Philippines, Andersen AFB, Guam, and Hickam AFB, Hawaii, was running four hours late. The pilots did not feel obligated to apologize to their passengers for the delay. When the purple Braniff jet finally climbed toward the brilliant stars in the expansive Hawaiian night, when the bland music had been turned off and the pleasant mini-skirted stewardesses had withdrawn after serving hot coffee to the grateful GIs, a hush fell over the dim cabinload of men. If they had thoughts of experiences past, of jungles or wounds or tedium, or if they had expectations of pleasures soon to come—a wife, a child, a stateside assignment, a home—the particular mix of each man became largely subliminal, merging with the comforting rush of the wind outside.

Only in the front compartment of the plane, usually reserved for general officers, did the scene vary slightly. There, accompanied by his escorts, in starched green fatigues without any markings of rank, a large white band with a prominent black S for "stockade" on his arm, Jonathan Bartlett watched the twinkling lights of Honolulu's finger communities fade into the distance. On his lap lay a book of Lin Yu Tang's to keep him company during the five-hour trip to the coast, his place marked by Maria's last one-line letter,

Dear Jon,
Be good in the clink, and come home soon.
Love, Maria

Perhaps in Kansas he could . . .